Afternoon suN

A NOVEL

SUSAN SURMAN

PROSPECTIVE PRESS LLC

1959 Peace Haven Rd, #246, Winston-Salem, NC 27106 U.S.A.
www.prospectivepress.com

Published in the United States of America by PROSPECTIVE PRESS LLC

TRADEMARK

AFTERNOON SUN

Cover and interior design by ARTE RAVE

ISBN 978-1-943419-37-1

First PROSPECTIVE PRESS trade paperback edition

Printed in the United States of America
First printing, November, 2016

1 3 5 7 9 10 8 6 4 2

The text of this book was typeset in Minion Pro
Accent text was typeset in Lithos Pro

PUBLISHER'S NOTE

Afternoon Sun

PART 1

No doubt it was on the veranda of Finca Vigia, *translated as 'outlook farm,' the home he bought outside Havana in 1940, when Ernest Hemingway, sipping a beer and puffing on a cigar said, "A writer should write what's burning up inside you."*

I have no idea where he uttered the words, but I did read somewhere he said them. Being a fan of Papa Hemingway's work, I always wanted to acknowledge his home in Havana, show off that I know it, even if it's just to me in my journal.

Burning up? I'm treading on hot coals. But maybe it's too soon. Maybe while you're smack dead in the middle of the crisis that's about to change your life, you can't produce as if by magic those words that make a sentence; the sentences that make a paragraph; paragraphs and chapters that make a book; dialogue that makes a play. Maybe because you don't know the ending. Maybe because it is too goddamn painful. Maybe because a writer has to write and you feel guilty if you don't. You read about how other authors make it through. No two do it the same way. I must just keep going until I pierce through the goddamn pain. Anything is better than nothing. Set a schedule. Two hours in the morning. Two hours in the evening. Do this for three weeks until it becomes a habit. It takes twenty-one days to make a new habit or break an old one. They've done research. Don't know who 'they' are. Then increase the two hours to three hours. Okay, so that's good. That's six hours a day of sitting in front of the screen. Something will come. There's no formula. It just takes the doing of it. It may not be what I will end up with, but it's the first draft of something. Verbal diarrhea. I'm a writer, not a social worker, a beautician, a fashion consultant, an actress, or a salesperson. Well, actually, I'm all those things. On paper.

A writer. Just the sound of it makes me tingle. When I have to fill out any forms and there's the line that requires something after occupation and I write 'Writer', I feel important. I feel validated. I feel like my life isn't a total waste. I'm contributing. I'm giving of myself. I'm using my natural gift. Maybe I'll be able to use some of this dribble later on. Write the first sentence. Anything. Dialogue, narrative, anything. It can be changed later. The heart is first. Then comes the head. Just get something down. Then use your chisel. Sculpt. Use music to set a mood.

My head knows all this. My heart is in the other room while my husband, soon to be ex-husband, is getting his stuff together because he is moving out because WE ARE IN THE THROES OF A SEPARATION WHICH WILL INEVITABLY LEAD TO DIVORCE. My first. His, too. Never again. And there's only one prerequisite for divorce. Marriage.

Write what's burning up inside you. Thank you, Papa Hemingway.

Working Titles: *In Between.*
Situation Wanted.

A play in two acts by Brenda
Gordon.

<u>BRIEF SYNOPSIS</u>: A Manhattan (or any major
city) separation/divorce in the works. The
Jordans are splitting up after ten (fifteen?)
years of marriage, no children, attempting to
face life as singles, fumbling, growing, not
growing, and mostly unable to let go of one
another even though they cannot live together.
They are in between.

<u>CAST OF CHARACTERS</u> (in order of appearance):
BRENDA JORDAN: 30's. A writer. Married to Ben.
BEN JORDAN: 30's. Successful real estate
broker.
JOSH: 30's. Brenda's first guy after the split
from Ben. Meets him jogging.
CAROL: 19. Ben's first. Meets her at the gym.
SELMA: Late 30's. Neighbor across the hall
from Ben in his new place.

SAMMY (V.O.): (Never seen). Selma's alcoholic/
drugged up husband.
MAID: Frumpy, any age. (Selma can double).

SETTING: Manhattan (or any major city) bedroom
of Ben and Brenda Jordan. The usual bedroom
furniture. Tasteful and mostly contemporary in
an eclectic kind of way.

TIME: The Present. Summer.

ACT ONE

AT RISE: BRENDA JORDAN sits at her desk
typing. Suddenly, she stops. She stares at
the screen. She taps out something. Hits the
delete key. Tries again. Deletes. Even though
it is summer, she wears an old flannel bathrobe
that has seen better days; fur bunny slippers
on her feet. A song by the velvet fog, Mel
Tormé, is playing, the TV is on but muted, the
telephone (a real phone) is ringing. Through
an open window, street noises are heard: a dog
barking, cars honking, children laughing and
screaming. With great force, the MAID ENTERS
pushing a very large and noisy vacuum. She
takes one look at the chaos, shouts "I QUIT"
and EXITS quickly neglecting to turn off the
vacuum. It is a few seconds before BRENDA
turns it off. The quiet is deafening.

And that's as far as Brenda had got on the play in several weeks with all that was being played out in her own life, never mind the lives of her embryonic characters. Unable to get any more than a working title, rough synopsis, cast list, setting, and description of the opening scene, no dialogue. Still, it was something. A little something is better than a lot of no something. Sometimes the title came after the work was written, so for now it wasn't a concern. Make it juicy, milk every emotion. That's what she wanted. She'd make it juicy, all right. Why invent? All she had to do was remember. But sometimes real life came out boring on paper. Use your imagination, kid. Embellish. That's the trick. How hard could it be if she put her mind to it? She had a gift. She knew that. She always knew that. She could write. It was just the doing of it. Solving the puzzle, as it were. When all was said and done, writing is about making decisions. The characters, their names, their relationships, their actions. What they want, what they do, where they live. And what they do to get there. Decisions. But it wasn't that easy. Convinced that a fifteen-year marriage had totally dulled her imagination, maybe this was a good thing that was happening now. Her mind would be clear to concentrate on her work. Making the transition was going to be tricky. She'd gone straight from a life in her parents' home to life with a husband.

Marriage. Mir-age. An optical illusion. How can you be so close, sleep together every night in the same bed for so many years, and before you know what's hit you, it all comes tumbling down. She was too young when they got married. They both were. They did what young couples do. The dating, the engagement, the sex, registering for wedding gifts, the china pattern, the sterling silver for show versus the stainless steel for longevity debate, the sex, the venue, the invitations, the bridal shower, the dress, the wedding ceremony and reception, the sex, the honeymoon (sea or mountains), the sex, the first apartment, the sex, furniture (contemporary or antique), in-laws, dinners and drinks for his business clients and prospects, cat or dog or fish or no pets, your friends, his friends, our friends, the sex. And then what?

Sex was now non-existent, neither one making any effort to change it. *Sexually Marooned* by Brenda Gordon. Good title for something. She didn't cheat. He didn't cheat. Well, as far as she knew he didn't. But she didn't think so. But she really didn't know. How does anyone know about anyone? Was it that she was just a lousy wife? She loathed cooking. She made the attempt, but it could never be called gourmet. She worked out, kept herself in shape, got manicures, pedicures, had a hair stylist, and employed a cleaning woman who came in once a week. Why wasn't that enough? Was she talking about her character, Brenda Jordan, or the real Brenda Gordon? Reality? Fantasy? How does an artist separate it? Was this at the crux of it? Men like regular and normal. She wasn't regular or normal. She had quirks. What about love? She loved him once. She really did. What happened? She believed he loved her. What happened? Maybe if she wore silky nightgowns to bed instead of t-shirts and shorts. Well, he wasn't exactly the son of a monarch in those cotton pajamas. Bermuda bottoms. With those knees peeking out the bottom of thigh-high pants.

In fifteen years, had Ben really been faithful? Why couldn't she believe that? She had been. Oh, maybe she looked once in a while. No harm in looking. But never once did any of those looks develop into more. Maybe a stolen kiss in the kitchen from a handsome guest at the party. A pat on the bottom from a neighbor at a backyard barbecue. She could see how easy it would be to cheat. But because some things in life had to mean something, she didn't act out any of the feelings she might have had. She was married. She had taken an oath at the wedding altar. Some things had to mean something.

From time to time, she couldn't help wondering about Ben, especially when he was late getting home from work. It would be easier for him. At the office. Out and about. Gorgeous women everywhere who made themselves available. Then there were the few times he bought her flowers for no reason and when she was sure she smelled perfume on his skin. When she wasn't being totally paranoid, she realized it was just his natural sweet smell. And when she hated herself most—those three or four times she went through his pockets looking for evidence. Evidence of what? And what would she have done if she found some incriminating piece of something? Piece of what? Create a scene? Demand an explanation? Cry? Scream? Walk out? Kick him out? Or do what the French women do—just go out and have your own affair.

Look the other way. Look the other way. Look the other way.

A messy attempt at a first draft of a novel provisional-ly titled *Sex Unzipped* was positively giving her the shakes, so she decided to leave it for a while and get on with the play. She could do that, work on two pieces at the same time. Sometimes, they got merged into one. When she felt stuck or bored with one, she'd go to the other. But that little system wasn't working. She was stuck. Period. Blocked is the professional term, which she absolutely loathed. Both the word itself and the activity; rather, the non-activity. If she could write now, it would be a catharsis and that would ease the real pain. Slightly easier to face the trials and tribulations of fictional characters than face your own demons.

On the other hand, in her heart of hearts, she was of the opinion that writing was the ultimate procrastination. The ultimate delay. Words, words, and more words. Procrasti-nation. A procrastination of life. Her life. And vice versa, because life, if you were living to the fullest, was the ulti-mate procrastination of putting words down on paper be-cause you are having such a grand time living. The creative curse. She often wished she'd been born with a clarinet in her mouth and that it was the only talent she had, without any doubts. Like Benny Goodman. Were there any female clarinet players? There must have been in those all girl orchestras during World War II.

Writing was hard. You had to be disciplined. You had to stay focused. How can you focus on such intense mental work when you're sorting your husband's socks in the drawer, doing his laundry, planning his meals, picking up his cleaning, meeting his business associates and their wives? All the wifely duties a wife is supposed to take on gladly because that's what marriage is. God! Her mother's words. When did they become hers? And now the new role of pretense. Pretending to be working, pretending not to be paying attention to him packing his things, pretending this wasn't moving day, pretending he wasn't moving out, pretending you haven't failed as a wife, pretending there will be life after a failed marriage. Just because you couldn't see it now didn't mean it wasn't out there. Did she really believe that?

Her parents never divorced. They were together until the end. What an ending. Even at the end, they were together. They'd been putting off for months going to see their financial advisor. Why this day in September? Why this particular September morning? She had to force herself to say the date. September 11, 2001. Why, why, why? Even now, from time to time, a wave came over her, and she wept for all the lost lives. For all the survivors. For the children growing up without parents. For her parents. For her loss. For the waste. A sudden thought brought her back to the present. The house keys. She and Ben always put their keys on the marble top table by the front door. What happens with the keys when he leaves the apartment? The final blow. The final cut. They never talked about it. Does he leave them? Does he take them? Does she ask for them? If he takes them, does she change the locks? Please take them so I don't hear them scrape across the top of the cold marble on the Italian table—next to the crystal vase of Japanese silk flowers and the Tiffany lamp. As she was getting older, she sounded more and more like her mother, who had been obsessed with name brands. Buy good stuff and it will last, she would say. Even after all the years, despite their differences at times, it was times like this when she wanted her mother more than anything. She wondered, if her mother were alive, would she be getting a divorce. Her mother loved Ben. He was the right man for her daughter. He would never stray. He would be there for the duration. Well, Mother, guess what!

So there she sat in their bedroom, soon to be her bedroom, at her desk in their Manhattan apartment, soon to be her apartment, overlooking Central Park. It was a wonderful apartment, and she was glad she was the one who was getting to stay in it. She went over to the window and looked across the street at the park. People of all ages walking and running in nothing more than skimpy shorts and t-shirts. What else would they wear? It was the middle of summer. And a very muggy one. Her husband kept the apartment like an igloo in summer. In winter, she kept it like a furnace. Mid-summer and she was freezing, so the warmth of a well-worn floor length flannel bathrobe wrapped around her body and furry slippers hugging her feet was comforting. Just like the Brenda character in her play. Art imitates life. Life imitates art. Which one is it? Is it both? Can it be both? This was really it. Moving day. There was that other moving day so very very long ago. She grabbed her journal, turned to a blank page and put pen to paper. A writer writes.

Remembering Moving Day. *My parents had gone ahead to the new apartment to wait for the arrival of the furniture while I stayed with my grandmother at the old apartment until everything was removed.*

The thick-set black man, called colored then, wore a tight-fitting white undershirt that allowed his muscle-proned body to loom out at anyone who might be looking. He'd been busy all morning. Now he halted in the doorway of my bedroom, looking beyond the wooden barrel sitting in the middle of the hardwood floor. The room was empty now except for the barrel and the little girl who was huddled in a corner of the room that had been her bedroom for all her seven years. The little girl was me. I was trembling with a wretched pathetic sobbing. Afraid to move, afraid to look at him, afraid to look away.

The moving man knew this sobbing. The white man's fear. The little girl would have heard the warnings from her mother. 'Colored people are bad. You mustn't talk to them. Except for Mildred. Mildred is different. She's very clean. She doesn't smell like a leather shoe.'

The moving man was Mildred's cousin. Mildred cleaned our apartment every other Friday. She talked to me like an adult. And I loved her. Mildred was all right. When I asked my mother to buy me a doll with a brown face, my mother was shocked. 'White children don't have chocolate babies.' And that was the end of that. When I told Mildred what my mother had said, she agreed and said my mother was right; that it was the same with her. She was never allowed to have a white doll when she was a child and it would never occur to her to buy a white doll for her little girl.

Still trembling and crying, I looked past the big colored moving man, across the living room to the kitchen where I could see my grandmother washing the last of our breakfast dishes in the sink, her back to the door. The cries of a child in desperate straits couldn't be heard by the deaf and dumb woman. In those days, it wasn't hearing impaired. If they couldn't hear or speak, they were deaf and dumb.

I held my breath as I watched the moving man walk through the living room area into the kitchen. Careful not to startle the old woman, he tapped lightly on her shoulder. Nana wasn't startled; surprised, but not startled. She turned away from the sink and looked up at him.

He brushed a finger over one of his eyes and exaggerating the words with his lips, he said softly, "Little girl cry." He pointed towards the bedroom. Towards me.

Nana followed his finger with her eyes and acknowledged the message with a nod. She dried her soapy hands on the dish towel hanging at the side of the sink and went quickly to her granddaughter. She couldn't speak, but managed a guttural sound like "no cry" that came from deep in her throat. I understood her. I always understood her.

Sometimes we would mouth the words, but we understood. It was a special bond we had. Using a corner of her apron, she wiped my tears. Taking my hand, she walked me into the kitchen while the moving man waited outside the room. I kept my head low so as not to make eye contact.

I was confused.

The man I thought was a bad man had been very kind to my grandmother. He knew not to frighten her. He knew to gently tap her shoulder. Most people were not so kind. Anyone with an affliction or deformity was mocked in our neighborhood. When Nana would take me out for a walk, the other children laughed and made faces at the old woman who could only grunt back at them. Even though she couldn't hear their mean words, she understood. She hadn't been born that way.

When I was old enough to understand, I was told that when my grandmother was five years old, she and her brother, two years older, came down with a bout of Scarlet Fever, and it left them both without speech or hearing. In the old days, it happened a lot like that. We had developed a way of communicating with hand gestures, sounds, mouthed words, sometimes writing the words on a piece of paper. For the rest of moving day, I stayed at Nana's side, sometimes sneaking glances over at the colored moving man, still afraid, and most of all hoping he didn't see me looking at him.

I loved my grandmother more than anyone. I think even more than I loved my mother and father. I never told that to anyone. It's the first time I've written it down.

Brenda could hear Ben puttering around in the next room, a second bedroom which had been transformed into a den. But she preferred her desk in the bedroom. They had many a discussion about it.

He: I can't understand why you work in the bedroom when we have this beautiful den.

She: It feels right.

He: Slightly inconvenient, wouldn't you say when I want to sleep and you want to write.

She: We could be in the middle of an inferno. You'd sleep through it.

He: Damned selfish, but have it your own way. You always do.

Somehow they worked it out. But not really. He bought her a laptop so she could move around; work in the other room at night. She hated it, claiming she couldn't think anywhere but in the bedroom and she couldn't get used to the keys on the laptop. Even when she learned that a regular keypad could be attached, she stuck to her guns.

He: You have all day to write when I'm out working.

She: Sometimes it doesn't come that way. You wouldn't understand.

He: That's right. I'm an idiot.

Preparing to leave the nest, he was. Their home. Their marriage. She was nearly thirty-eight years old and had gone straight from living with her parents to life with Ben. She'd never been alone. She had never wanted to do anything but write. Marriage to Ben gave her the luxury without her having to work at a job. He had told her he would support them while she did her thing. Money was never the problem. He'd joined his father's firm and made a splash when real estate was the way to go. That's how they met. Her mother and father had come into some money from a cousin who had no children and they wanted to move into the city from Brooklyn. They were looking for a modest sized apartment on the Lower East Side. Enter Ben Gordon who said he could get them a much better deal on the Upper East Side. Her mother made sure Brenda was with them the second time they came in contact with Ben.

"A match made in heaven," her mother said.

"Marriages may be made in heaven but they have to be lived on earth," her father said.

"Shush!"

Her mother couldn't have been happier. About Ben, that is. Ben Gordon was a real catch according to the sheltered woman's knowledge of men which came strictly from romance novels and romantic comedy.

One date led to another and two years later, there was a wedding. During the first part of this relationship, it hadn't been totally exclusive with Ben. She wasn't proud of this because it meant sneaking around which was totally draining.

She developed an ulcer.

Out of college, her parents wanted to give her a gift. Ben hadn't yet become quite ensconced, so Brenda jumped at the chance to go to Paris for seven days. A whole week in Paris.

No longer that little girl on moving day, but still slightly fearful of men of color, now called black or African American, it was a chance meeting. Unless you believe that nothing is a coincidence. At first, it was her chance to overcome prejudices she harbored. Until it became more.

It happened that they were seat partners on the flight from New York to Paris and began to talk as soon as they boarded and didn't stop until they arrived at their destination and not even then. They continued their plane chatter, only now it wasn't just plane chatter, in the city of light as they took in the museums, the cafés, the restaurants, art galleries, sometimes letting their hands brush together as if by accident as they strolled along the banks of the Seine.

He was handsome with strong features. He was charming. He was well-spoken. He was intelligent. He was eight years older than she. People were color blind to a professor who taught English Literature at New York University and who was a published author. He was fun to be with. She didn't resist. And she was far from home. She gave herself permission to explore this new adventure. Free to discover parts of her she didn't know existed. Their different skin pigmentations didn't exist, not for them, or for anyone in this city. She had never felt this way about any other man. And certainly not Ben whom her parents adored and were expecting a serious liaison between their daughter and him. But really, it was because she was feeling differently about herself. Boundaries fell. She became who she was with this man. Is this what freedom feels like? Freedom to love and be loved? She felt...she hesitated not sure of the word...alive. She felt alive with this man whose skin was a different color than hers. He fell in love, and she did, too.

They continued their relationship back home in New York. Because she didn't want to be talked out of this love, for a long time she kept him a secret from family and friends. Only once did he refer to it, during a mild disagreement about something trivial, later apologizing. "Does your mother know you're sleeping with a black man?" He hadn't asked it to get an answer. He knew the answer.

She met his mother who had brought him up on her own after his father had taken off to points unknown. An open-minded, way ahead of the curve, extremely bright liberal woman who happened to be a beauty, she kept company with men of all nationalities and embraced her son's lover.

And then the holiday season was upon them and the little girl, who was all grown up now, decided it wasn't going to be a secret anymore. She brought him to her parents' apartment for Thanksgiving. Her father had an instant rapport with the man his daughter loved. Her mother's behavior was transparent, almost embarrassing, and certainly less than gracious. Never looking directly at him, she blabbed on about the food, the table décor, all the Thanksgivings she'd had as a kid and as an adult. She recited her recipe for cranberry relish handed down from her grandmother, except Brenda knew it wasn't her grandmother's handed down recipe. It came from some website.

Her assessment of the event, meaning of him, Nathan, came a few days later. Given her own upbringing and what she had spoon-fed her daughter, her opinion was only slightly veiled because finally, she was coming face to face with what she really felt. To her daughter, she said snidely, "I suppose he could be called good looking. Handsome, really. A nice color. You know. Not dark. I once had a jacket that color. Not black black. Not brown, either. Like black coffee with three teaspoons of cream. Like Lena Horne. That's the color. Didn't she have beautiful skin? Did she die?"

"And Happy Thanksgiving to you, too, Mother. By the way, Nathan and I will be spending Christmas with his mother."

"Does he know you're Jewish?"

"I don't think it has come up in conversation."

"And what about Ben Gordon? That's the type you marry if you want any kind of a real life."

"Why can't you just let me be happy?"

"You didn't tell me what you thought of the cranberry relish."

"It was a nice color. Not too orange, not too red." And those were the last words she said for a while because they didn't talk for months.

And then they talked. And Ben Gordon, whom Mother adored for her daughter, always seemed to be around. And eventually, exit Nathan. He'd been offered a job in Vietnam teaching English and said he couldn't refuse. It was the polite way of telling Brenda it was over. Mother was relieved. In a way, maybe Brenda was, too. It had been a whirlwind romance fostered in Paris and had run its course. They'd always have Paris, as the saying goes. How more romantic can you get than that? She'd been in love for a little while, or thought she was, and it was pretty wonderful. Whoever said love and marriage went together didn't know what they were talking about. Oh. That was a song. Just a song.

Looking immaculate and, in Brenda's opinion, rather overdressed for the occasion, in beige slacks, a light-weight navy sports jacket, and a light blue shirt, Ben tiptoed quickly into the bedroom.

Brenda studied him. Jesus. Now he's Fred Astaire. Doesn't have a care in the world. Isn't that the shirt I bought him? Nice shirt. Only Ben would wear a sports jacket to divide the personal contents of the household.

Idiot.

He was always the neat one, dedicated to the nitty gritty details in life. In a certain light, while not what one would describe as handsome, he was quite good looking. If she squinted, she could see Kirk Douglas. Or was it Michael. One of them. On closer scrutiny, he was no Hollywood look-alike. Just Mister Ben Manhattan Real Estate Stock Market Playing Gordon.

And then she smiled, remembering her mother's description of less fortunate looking men. "He makes a nice appearance," she would say. You knew right away that meant a face and build like Shrek. Brenda had known a few of those before Ben came along.

The phone came alive with a piercing ring, Brenda not moving. Ben gave her the look that says, 'Well, answer it.'

The phone kept ringing until finally he picked up, giving her the look that says, 'Why didn't you answer?' One thing you get out of marriage is that shorthand.

"Yes? Gordon here," he said.

"Not hello, like a normal person," she said.

Judging from his winces, the other end was highly censorable.

He grunted and slammed down the receiver. "If it rings again, don't answer."

Brenda said nothing.

Sure enough, it rang again.

Ignoring his instructions, she answered. "Hello?"

Ben just threw his hands up in the air.

"Hello," she repeated.

"What color panties are you wearing?" The man's voice was low and seductive.

"I haven't any on." Brenda held out the receiver so Ben could hear the other end. To Ben she said, "I think it's for you."

Ben rolled his eyes upwards.

"What color bra are you wearing?" said the caller.

"I'm not wearing a bra."

"HANG UP, BRENDA," Ben shouted.

"Haven't you anything on?" the voice asked.

"Only my husband. Wanna talk to him?"

Silence.

"Hello, caller? Are you still there?" She waited. Nothing. Even though he wasn't there, she said, "Please state your occupation, financial assets, and availability. I'm getting divorced." She hung up.

"You're nuts, Brenda. Boy, are we doing the right thing."

"Amazing how powerful that word is, isn't it? Husband. It works better than mace. Maybe that should be mice."

Ben stomped off to the other room.

Half to him, half to herself, Brenda said, "Don't go away mad. Just go away."

What had brought him into the bedroom in the first place? It wasn't the ringing phone and it certainly wasn't her. Or was it? And anyway, he could have picked up in the other room. They had phones all over the apartment. Landlines, a variety of cell phones, mobile phones. They were well-endowed, phone-wise.

She felt numb. Good word. Numb. It reminded her why she was sitting at the desk. She minimized the play and brought up the half-written novel. "Sex Unzipped, a novel in English by Brenda Gordon," she read aloud.

It always sounded different reading it aloud. Not always better; just different. As if someone else had written it. A good way to pick up the flaws. The jagged edges, she called it. That's how she saw it. A smooth triangle, but if something wasn't working, rough edges jutted out from the otherwise smooth triangle. That's when she knew she had a lot of re-writing and editing to do. Writing was re-writing.

"By Brenda Gordon," she repeated. "A novel in English."

Nice touch. Unnecessary, but she liked it. Anyway, she'd deal with it later. It was unimportant. Just another procrastination.

She read, "Valentino smelled her hair, her neck, her hands. He licked her face, her elbows. He kissed her nose. He slid his finger over her big toe in Red Burgundy nail polish. Gloss. With great feeling, he asked, 'Who the hell are you, Maxine?' Maxine looked him straight in the eye, and right to his face—"

The telephone's ring interrupted her. She waited, letting it ring, noting, but not acknowledging, Ben coming in the room juggling his laptop. The laptop meant they would be continuing the discussion about the separation of household goods.

He picked up the receiver. "Yes?"

He listened.

"What? Who the hell is this?" His mouth hung open. "What did you say? I dare you to repeat that!"

If he'd shown that much passion in bed, maybe we wouldn't be getting a divorce, Brenda thought.

Deliberately, cunningly overlapping her novel's dialogue with his phone dialogue, she continued reading her work aloud. "…and right to his face, man to man, spat out something her godfather had taught her. *Che cazzo vuoi da me vattene perche ti rompom le balle. Capito?*"

"What are you after prick? I'll cut your balls off," snapped Ben. A perfect translation of her Italian slang, it was sheer accident because he didn't understand Italian. The timing was impeccable. Utterly infuriated, Ben practically pushed the receiver through its cradle.

"My, my. So Continental."

"If that sonofabitch calls again, call the police. Okay, let's get this list over with. Continue from where we left off. Where were we?" He looked at the phone. "Pervert. I've a good mind to call the phone company. Are you set up?" He pointed to her computer.

"Getting there." She found the document. Inventory of Household Contents and Personal Effects. His list. Her list. What a world. They were standing next to each other, and they were communicating through technology.

When she was sure he had stopped his verbal rampage, she answered his question matter-of-factly about where they were. "Music. We were on the music section." She didn't want him to think she was making an issue out of it. Why? Because she was dead, that's why.

He sat down on the upholstered bench at the foot of their bed and with laptop on his lap, did the necessary scrolling and found his list.

"Ahmad Jahmal. It's like a goddamn oven in here. Did you adjust the air?" He slipped off his jacket.

She scrolled down.

"Under the CDs section," he added.

"I know where it is. You didn't even know Ahmad Jahmal before me."

Ignoring the statement, he said, "We made a deal, Brenda. One Ahmad for two Dukes."

"One Duke Ellington is enough. Besides, according to my list, I'm getting two Duke Ellingtons for two Erroll Garners."

She studied her screen.

"No, no. If you recall, Brenda, the two Errolls were mine originally."

"Originally, Ben, you had records and albums like everybody else, and we didn't communicate by computers while in the same room, but be that as it may." She waved a hand in the air.

"We should really be texting. Much more convenient."

"Tell ya what, Ben. You can have Dinah Washington."

"Keep her. What happened to the drum solos? Gene Krupa? Buddy Rich?"

"On the list."

"You know what I mean."

"But you like Dinah Washington." One very major thing they had in common was the type of music they liked.

"I can't find the drum solos. I looked all over the apartment. You assume I like Dinah because I never said I didn't."

"Threw it away," she replied defiantly.

"What do you mean exactly by threw it away?"

"The time I had the flu."

He had to think a minute. "When you smashed the one radio we had against the mirror. That was charming. I remember."

"You want charming? I had a hundred and three temperature, and you left me alone for fifteen hours. That's what I call charming."

"I was working, Brenda."

"On the golf course. In the dark."

With each barb, their voices grew higher and shriller.

"You don't throw away music. Damn you, Brenda. You threw out drum solos. There were drum solos on that CD. My favorites. Gene Krupa. Buddy Rich. Sid Catlett."

"All dead. You're up on technology. Ever hear of YouTube?"

"I'm taking Lena Horne."

"As long as you leave me Frank Sinatra."

"One Frank. One. I've got the other three."

"I want Madison Square Garden!"

"Jesus, Brenda, you're getting the apartment!"

"One apartment. Check."

And with great aplomb, to put a point on it, she marked a huge bold X on her list. It should have been a check mark, but the keys weren't so equipped. Their voices had reached the summit, couldn't go any higher if they were at La Scala. They each took a breath. After a slight pause, Ben opened with a new subject. "What happened to my dirty laundry?"

"I don't seem to have that number on my list. Dave Brubeck?"

"Great time for jokes." Except he wasn't laughing.

"No dirty laundry."

"You sent it out?"

"Laundromat. Don't worry. I boiled your handkerchiefs. Why can't you use Kleenex like everybody else?"

"Not everyone has my problem."

"It's your diet I keep telling you."

"Lay off. It isn't my diet. I have a good diet. Did you iron the handkerchiefs?"

"Did you know you have a total of seventy-two hand-kerchiefs?"

"I use three a day, sometimes four. You knew that when you married me. You know who keeps buying me handker-chiefs."

"She keeps buying me chocolate covered prunes. Tell your mother you don't want any more handkerchiefs. And I don't want any more prunes."

"I can't even tell her we're getting a divorce."

And there it was. Out loud. The word that described what they were doing. The bell announcing round one was over. But if all the arguments could be counted since the be-ginning, because they knew a split was on the horizon, this was closer to round fifty-one.

He pulled out a clean white handkerchief from his pants pocket, shook it out slowly and blew his nose with great aplomb.

"Oh no, here it comes. The handkerchief trick. You make a feature of that goddamn catarrh of yours. We go into a restaurant and just before you sit down, out comes the handkerchief. It's embarrassing. And not very sanitary."

"Well, you aren't going to have to worry about it anymore."

He meticulously folded the handkerchief so the unused section remained on the outside and stuffed the hankie back into his pocket.

"It's your diet, I keep telling you," she said calmly.

"My diet's fine. Oh, shit," he hollered.

She jumped. "Don't do that. What? What?"

"The boxes in the storage room in the basement. Why aren't they on the inventory?" He scrolled down. "Shit."

"Well I guess we just forgot in all the excitement and all."

"I won't have room in the new place. I'll just have to leave them for now. Mostly Business Administration text books. Stuff from high school."

They went back and forth a little longer until the entire inventory had been covered, checked off, and the whole deal was tied up. Mine, yours, no more ours.

Title: *The End of a Marriage.*

It was late afternoon when he left the apartment; attempt-ed to leave the apartment, that is. A slight case of hyper-ventilation as she lay on the bed delayed his departure. She literally thought she was going to die. She couldn't move. She couldn't remember ever feeling this frightened or help-less. She thought she might faint.

"What are you doing?" he asked with all the compassion of a donkey.

"Ben, wait. I...I...can't catch my breath."

He hesitated in the doorway. "Stop this."

"Ben," she gasped. "I can't...."

He closed his eyes a second before going to her. "Stoppit, dammit. You're doing this on purpose. Breathe, Brenda. Just breathe. Take slow deep breaths. You know how to breathe, don't you?" He sat down on the bed. "We both agreed. We have talked and talked about it. In five words: We can't be married anymore."

"I can't...can't...." She couldn't take in any air.

"Stop talking. Breathe, take slow deep breaths. Come on. In. Out."

He had his arm around her. When was the last time he had even touched her? Where was a paper bag when you needed one? Somehow, slowly, her breathing became normal. He moved away, unsure whether to leave or stay longer. He got her a glass of water.

She sat up. "Thanks."

"Small sips."

She took the glass and sipped the water. She still felt as if she was going to die. She wanted to. She prayed for it.

"One of us has to move out. We've gone over and over this. We agreed it was easier if I was the one."

"I know. I know."

"Come on, Bren. Be a big girl. This isn't easy for me, either."

"Be a big girl. Have you any idea how insulting you are? Well, go. Just go. I hand you over on a silver platter."

"What are you talking about?"

"You must have someone you're going to. Men don't just leave. They go to someone."

"There isn't anyone, Brenda. There never has been."

"Then why? Why?"

"We've been over this a million times. I can't give you what you want. You can't give me what I want."

"We used to."

"Needs change."

"That simple?"

"That simple. No, it isn't simple. How the hell do I know? We can't be together, that's all I know. You can get on with your novel now or your play or whatever you're doing."

"You mean my semi-autobiographical biographical play? Half-truth, half-lie, and half-done." Venom poured out of her with every word. She no longer had to be the nice one.

"I didn't mean to open up a can of worms."

"I see a freshly snowed on hill. I roll around and bleed on it. I want my blood to stain that white peaceful place before anyone turns it into gray slush."

"What movie did you get that from?"

She said nothing. She didn't need to be the one to fill in the space. So the words stayed unsaid. For about a second.

"You can hang yourself for all I care," she said finally.

"Look, Bren, I think we hit bottom a long time ago. Everything's a crisis with you."

"Ha! You lose! I win!"

"What are you talking about? Lose? Win? Up and down. Up and down. Maybe you're bi-polar. See a doctor."

"You liked that manic-depressive thing about me in the beginning."

"True, but you were quieter about it."

"I'm fighting for my life, damn you!"

"I'm fighting for my life, too. The only difference between us is, you cry out loud and I cry inside. I'm hurting too, you know, Brenda. We can't keep doing this. It's done. We decided. We've been through it. We know what we have to do."

"Really no one else?"

"No one. I swear."

"Will you get married again?"

"Jesus, Brenda, the body isn't even cold yet. How the hell should I know? I can't even get out of the apartment. There might be someone else for you, too. It's a possibility. We can't talk about this now. You decide for you. And I'll decide for me. We aren't a couple. Get it through your head."

"I don't want to be old and alone."

"How do you know? You might like being single."

"I'm frightened. You always took care of the money side of things."

"I'll take care of you financially. You know that. You can do anything you want. You don't have to worry about money. Give it a chance. You might love the whole bachelorette thing."

"Right now, I hate it."

"It's too soon. I haven't left yet."

"Ben?"

"Yes?"

"I think you should go now."

He sighed heavily, turned, and walked quickly out of the room.

She stayed in the bedroom. No goodbye. Not even a muffled bye. She waited for the sound of the keys. Front door closing, no keys hitting the marble table. He hadn't left the keys. She sat frozen, the only words in her head: Begin to reconstruct. Begin to reconstruct.

Now she'd only have to take care of herself. She could go back to school. Take classes at the college. Maybe teach. Immerse herself in her writing. Swim in the words. Her words.

Freedom. Go back to her maiden name of—what was her maiden name? Oh…Glimcher. The monogrammed guest towels and pillow cases and dinner napkins with the fanciful embroidered *G* could remain in her possession. Chalk it up to more stuff. Goody. Upon reflection, perhaps best to keep the name Gordon. Looks better on the front cover of a book and on a screen credit. Definitely Gordon. She was only glad her mother wasn't alive to witness all this decay. But that was another story. She couldn't even think about it. Not today. Dora Glimcher believed in one marriage for life. Even if you couldn't stand each other. Were Dora and Herb Glimcher in love? Did they even like each other? One marriage. Even in death. The partner who remained living mustn't marry again. That's what they believed. It never became an issue because they both …both…went together.

On the other hand, Brenda's older sister, Eve, didn't follow that philosophy. She was on her fourth husband and currently living in Italy. No, wait, that was number three. Paolo. His name meant small in English. Brenda had looked it up. No need to develop that scenario further. They weren't married very long. Number four is the Greek. Demetrius. The charmed number four. The last Brenda heard, they were living just outside Athens. Or was it Sicily? Brenda couldn't keep up. Brenda smiled when she recalled that Eve's first was named Adam. Go figure. She drew a blank on number two's name.

Maybe she needed her big sister now. And maybe not. When the parents, the glue that held the family together, died, the two sisters more or less became estranged. They talked about doing the Skype thing, but never got around to it. A very occasional e-mail was their only contact. For a while, Eve was big on Facebook, but Brenda wasn't really interested in social media. She didn't cry. She wanted to, but the tears wouldn't come. She wrote for a while. Just some scribbles. Poetry. Longhand on a yellow legal pad. Slightly more intimate than on a computer. She pondered for a while. Wrote a little. Thought. Wrote. Thought. Less painful to cry on paper. A writer writes. She was teaching herself Haiku.

> *When fall comes knocking*
> *Will we be open to life's*
> *Possibilities*

The days went by slowly. She never left the apartment. All food was ordered and brought in by delivery men. She and Ben talked on the phone every other day. Were they really better apart than together? Too soon to know. He didn't seem to have a problem letting her know what he was doing. She had nothing to report. Her lackluster life spurred her on. She tapped away at those keys as if her life depended on it. She still didn't have a title for the play, but that would come. And she wasn't sure about the names. Jordan was too much like Gordon. Maybe Ben and Brenda Jordan wasn't the way to go. She could decide that later.

Lights up on Ben Jordan's studio apartment. Ben is in bed with Carol, a much younger woman.

They heave about on top of the covers.

CAROL

He won't give me a divorce. I'm gonna kill myself. And then I'm gonna kill you.

(Telephone rings)

Don't answer.

BEN

I see those acting lessons are paying off. Might be important. I have to answer. (Into phone) Hello?

BRENDA

Ben?

(CAROL disappears under the covers)

                    BEN

Carol! Stop it, will you! I'm on the phone.

                    BRENDA

(On the phone) Is this Ben Jordan?

                    BEN

Yes. Who is this?

                    BRENDA

Ben, it's me. Brenda. Brenda. Your soon-to-be-ex.

                    BEN

Oh, that Brenda.

                         (Distracted by the duffel bag
                         he spots on the floor for the
                         first time)

(To Carol) What's that bag?

                    BRENDA

Beg your pardon?

                    CAROL

You told me to bring over my stuff.

                    BEN

A brown paper shopping bag, not your whole house.

                    BRENDA

Ben!

                    BEN

Brenda!

                    BRENDA

Are you okay?

                    BEN

Fine, fine, fine. How are you?

                    BRENDA

I think I better call back.

                    BEN

No, no. What's wrong? Is something wrong?

                         (CAROL comes up for air)

It's Brenda, my ex-wife. Soon to be ex.

                    CAROL

I'm thrilled.

                         (LIGHTS UP on BRENDA)
                    BRENDA

Ben?

                    BEN

Brenda?

                    BRENDA

Ben, a couple of men are here.

                    BEN

That's great. Good for you.

                    BRENDA

From the TV rental company saying there's money
owed or they take the set away. What should I
do?

                    BEN

I knew we should have bought instead of rented.
I paid it to the end of the year. They got their
records screwed up.

                         (CAROL dives under the covers
                         again. BEN howls)

Your feet are freezing, Carol!

                    BRENDA

Pardon? What did you say?

                    BEN

I've been wheezing. Like Ray Farrell. In my
office.

                    BRENDA

Somebody's there.

                    BEN

No, nobody. A friend.

                         CAROL (Sticking her head out)

Friend of those who have no friends.

                    BEN

Shut up! This woman has a crisis on her hands.

                    CAROL

So have I. In a minute.

                         (Dives under the covers)

                    BEN

(To CAROL) The TV people are ready to drag the
set out.

                    CAROL

                         (Sticks her head out a second)

No way. They don't do that.

                    BEN

Brenda doesn't lie.

                    CAROL

Color?

                         (Under the covers again)

                    BEN

Of course color. You think she'd be this upset
over black and white?!

                    BRENDA

Ben! Hello? Ben!

                    BEN

Calm down. Calm down. How much do they want?

                    BRENDA

All of it.

                    BEN

And Brenda, is it the black and white or the
color?

                    BRENDA

Black and white?

                    BEN

Black and white.

                    BRENDA

Sold it.

                    BEN

You don't own a rented set to sell it. How much?

                    BRENDA

Fifty.

                    BEN

You should have called me if you needed money.

                    BRENDA

I did. Your secretary said you couldn't be
disturbed.

                    CAROL
                    (Comes up for air)

Goodbye, Brenda!

                    (BEN and CAROL struggle with
                    the phone. BRENDA hangs up.
                    LIGHTS OUT on HER)

BEN

(Into phone) You can call anytime. I'd get an unlisted number if I didn't want you to call, wouldn't I? I'll always be here for you. It's just gonna take time to get used to the new arrangement, that's all. Just give the guys a postdated check and I'll call them on Monday and take care of it. Okay? Brenda? Brenda? (Hangs up) She hung up.
She sold a rented TV that was in my name. Can you believe
that?

CAROL

You're divorced, Ben. When are you going to let go?

BEN

It isn't final yet.

CAROL

You're still in love with her.

BEN

You don't understand. She's family.

CAROL

So why didn't you stay married?

BEN

I'm not prepared to have this conversation now.

CAROL

I thought you and I—well, you know.

                    BEN

Gee, Carol, I'm sorry. I'm not even divorced
yet.

                    CAROL

But I thought, you know. You, me.

                    BEN

It isn't like that with you and me. With anyone.

                    CAROL

What is it?

                    BEN

I'm nowhere right now. No one is.

                    CAROL

You call me when you need my body. I feel used.

                    BEN

Friends don't use each other. You can call me,
too.

                    CAROL

You're an A-1 turd. You're all alike. Animals.

                    BEN

You don't really mean that. You're a very sweet
girl.

                    CAROL

Thanks.

                    BEN

There are guys who would go through shit for
you.

                    CAROL

Pigs. All of you.

                    BEN

This sex thing with you might be a vitamin
deficiency.

                    CAROL

You're so lame, it isn't funny.

                    BEN

I'm serious. Could be lack of vitamin D.

                    CAROL

Do you know how many vitamins I swallow every
day?

                    BEN

Maybe they're the wrong ones.

                    CAROL

A, B, C, D, E, cal-mag, fish oil, curcumin,
enzymes.

                    BEN

That's a lot of pills.

                    CAROL

I have a nutritionist. It's a metabolic thing.

BEN

All I'm saying is your excessive need for sex could be related to vitamins, curable by the correct supplements. Operative word: correct.

CAROL

Cure it? Cure it? I want to triple it!

BEN

Ah, youth. Sometimes I need to talk. Just talk. I like you. And the truth is I like being seen with you.

CAROL

I like being obscene with you.

BEN

I'm asking you to be my friend.

CAROL

Are you gay?

BEN

I am not gay. I feel at ease with you. Lie back.

CAROL

You found a new way to do it?

BEN

I just need to talk sometimes.

                    CAROL

So talk.

                    BEN

As I get older, I'm discovering that I'm much
more interesting than everyone else.

                    CAROL

And here we are worried about my vitamin intake.

                    BEN

So what do you think?

                    CAROL

You could try not talking to anyone.

                    BEN

People won't leave me alone. In my profession,
you have to be likable. It's this state of flux.
It's killing me. I need a regular life.

                    CAROL

Like regular sex?

                    BEN

That isn't that important. I mean, it's
important, just not the major thing.

                    CAROL

What about irregular sex?

                    BEN

I've got a real problem.

CAROL

Viagra. It works on television.

BEN

No, not that.

CAROL

Do you want to know what bugs me?

BEN

Sure. It's a conversation. Two-way. Go.

CAROL

I'm getting fat. I can't stand my body. My ass.

BEN

It's very nice.

CAROL

Trust me. It's too low. I mean if it's like this now, what's it gonna be like when I'm twenty-five?

BEN

I believe they have special diets and exercises for that area. I'll ask Brenda. She knows some great diets.

CAROL

Yeah, she's good at losing weight.

BEN

I told you this before?

CAROL

She lost you, shit for brains.

BLACKOUT

END OF SCENE.

The play was pouring out of her. Brenda wrote until she couldn't write anymore. Weeks of writing. How many hours, how many weeks since he'd walked out the door? It felt like it had happened eons ago. Was it all a dream? Had it really happened? He went out for a newspaper. That's all. He'll be back. But she knew better. Was she getting a message that she really loved him? She needed a sign, a message. Still loved him? Never stopped loving him? She listened to the silence. It was deafening. There was no message. She wondered how she would really feel if what she wrote was true.

The ringing phone was a shock. So quiet, so still, and then this loud clanging. A gentleman caller, perchance? To answer or not to answer. Why all the fuss? Thanks to caller ID, it was Benjamin Alan Gordon, aka BAG to his friends and enemies. In his business, he must harbor lots of enemies. Was it a sign? Calmly, or was it with anticipation, maybe hope, or anger, or disgust, or fear or…for chrissakes, Brenda, just pick up.

"Pronto."

"Ah. Your Italian phase."

He talked.

She listened.

He talked some more.

She listened some more. Then she gave it to him good.

"Hold on there, buster. Do you really think I am going to do your bidding at this stage of the game? Do you really think you can vacate the premises and then call me up and ask me to do your errands? We have split up. We are getting a divorce. What is it about the concept of the phrase 'split up' that you don't understand? Are you listening, Benjamin? Have you expired? I don't hear any breathing."

"I'm here." He let out a sigh.

"The sigh. I thought that was my trick." As if she were talking to a child, she went on pointedly, "Actually, Ben, I don't think that type of thing is in my job description now that we are no longer together. You will just have to make your own arrangements with Mr. Saul Chadwick, your business colleague from out of town. I'm not calling him for you. I don't care if he has to rent a park bench to sleep on. I'm not going to arrange a hotel for him. I am no longer your secretary. Or your housekeeper. Or your cook." She wasn't getting divorced to spend more time with him.

But as soon at the words slipped from her tongue, she knew she would do it all. She'd set up the meeting with Chadwick. She'd book a hotel. She'd meet Ben for lunch if he asked. Or for dinner. She'd meet him at their favorite restaurant, the one where he first proposed. They would go out on dates. The theatre. The ballet. The opera. Museums. She'd invite him over and cook his favorite meal. She'd go back to the auburn tinted hair he liked so much. Sometimes they will sleep together. They will hold hands when they sign the final divorce papers. They will both cry. And it wouldn't stop until one of them met someone else. Maybe not even then. They were lousy together; maybe they'd be better apart. Can't live with you, can't live without you. They were in between. And there it was. The working title of her play. In Between.

Good title.

"Ben? Ben! You still there? Ben?"

"Yuh."

"How's your, you know, the place?"

"It'll do for now. I need furniture. Maybe I'll send some-one for the pull-out couch in the den. If that's okay. I know it wasn't on the list."

"Yuh. Sure. Sure. Okay."

Then there was a long silence. He was crying. She could taste his tears. She began, too. Not loud sobbing. A soft moaning. She felt worse for him than for herself. How twist-ed was that.

"Listen, Ben. Never mind what I said. I'll make the call for you. What time should I tell Chadwick to meet you?"

No reply.

"Ben?"

He'd hung up. She got it. It was never intended to be a chatty type call. And it wasn't about Saul Chadwick, busi-ness colleague. It was just to let her know he was thinking of her. To see if she was okay. To let her know he was all right. What a stinking business, it all was. Good and stinking.

She emptied a glass of red, maybe two or three, no one was counting, with each swallow enjoying the fruity taste more, feeling empowered, feeling mellow, feeling no feel-ing. She grabbed a wedge of Edam cheese from the fridge, the first bite of food all day. She wasn't sure. Maybe she had eaten earlier. Lamps were turned on. Too much light. She dimmed them. The soft glow should have made her feel pretty. She felt lousy.

Because she was alive, still rake thin, still attractive, not broke, not yet divorced, still Mrs. Gordon, she felt, what? Not happy. Not happy. Content? Actually, she had no idea how she felt. Breaking up was hard to do. She would move to Paris, live in a garret in *Saint Germain Des Pres*, eat snails, and write poetry in a café on the Left Bank. Everyone went to Paris. Maybe not. Tuscany. Much better. Tuscany. Been there, done that. Israel? Too Jewish. Greece? Corfu or Crete. Perfect. No! That's where sister Eve was supposedly now living with husband number four. One of those places.

The hell with it. All of it. More wine. Forget a glass. Put a nipple on the bottle.

She wrote until dawn. What came out surprised her. She didn't understand it, but she liked it. A kind of a poem. She would use it in something later on. A writer writes.

```
Saul loved the way her long slender fingers
fiddled
with the New York Times crossword puzzle;
He loved being secretly in love with Lola;
She was sixteen
High school prom queen;
Saul was Jewish
She was the other;
His mother (how did she find out) screamed,
"Your tongue will fall out of your head."
"I thought you go blind," he replied
"No! That's the other thing, God forbid."
After that, Saul was home-schooled;
All locks were removed from bathroom,
bedroom, and closet doors;
Saul grew up and
married a nice Jewish girl
from the same neighborhood;
They had a son
named Leonard
who
in time
openly
became Lenore.
And that's what happens
when you don't have locks
on your doors.
```

Then she went to bed.

The worst thing about death, the very worst thing when someone you have loved or liked or been married to dies, is opening your eyes after a sleep. The waking up. That's the worst part. You wake up, still too groggy to have complete comprehension, the fogginess dissipates after a few seconds, and the reality hits. You are still alive. That person is never coming back. You have to get through another day. The emptiness washes over you. That empty hollow feeling that you think will never go away. You don't recognize who you are. Drag yourself to the kitchen. Make coffee. Distracted, you put tea leaves in the coffee pot. Where are you? In the kitchen. You don't remember how you got to the kitchen. Weren't you just in the bedroom? You are so dizzy, you will fall if you don't grab the back of the kitchen chair or lean on the kitchen table. He's dead. But you can't say the word; can't even think it. He isn't here anymore. You try to identify what you feel. For fifteen years you've waited to hear those words. He's dead. You ask why him. Wasn't he the strong one? What if you had made that call that day. If you had been kinder the last time he wanted to see you. After the final decree. All the what-ifs. Was he that unhappy? He was taking anti-depressants. Did that cause the chemical imbalance?

And you have mornings and mornings of it. Days and days. And nights. The nights are the worst. You can never forget the scene. He's sitting in a meeting, walks over to the closed window, opens the window, looks at the street seven, eight stories below. Not anything to attract the attention of the members of the board. Before anyone knows what's happening, he goes out the window. It takes a second before the moans and the oh my gods and the what's happening? Ben? He's the last person to do that. Splat. Beige suit, white shirt, blue tie. Cars screech to a halt. Passersby don't know whether to stop or keep walking; in either case, averting their eyes from the tragic scene. It looks different in real life. In real life, you have to look away. Not like a movie or on TV. On TV you can watch the brutality. But not here, right now on the pavement in front of you. Virtual reality. Step away. You might get blood on your shoes and because it's summer, on your toes peeking out from your sandals. So you keep moving, maybe look up to where it began, the window ledge, but not so anyone can see. And you keep moving. And you read about it in the papers the next day. If you're a night owl, see it on the news that night.

Brenda bolted upright in bed, drenched in a cold sweat. It was the worst dream she had ever ever ever had in her life. Not a dream. A nightmare. As vivid as any real life experience. There was no face, so was it Ben? Is that what she secretly wanted? Ben's death? Much easier to deal with than divorce. Death is final. Divorce never ends. A dream. Only a dream. Is death better than divorce? Divorce is a kind of death.

She had to phone him. Had to hear his voice. He wasn't taking calls his secretary said. No, no message. They hadn't had any communication in almost two months. It felt like her right arm had been severed. No! No! No! She was going to get through this. She was going to stand on her own two feet. She was going to learn how to do the bills, get her own insurance, do everything without Ben. His money she wouldn't say no to. That foolish she wasn't. It was much easier to be independent when you had some financial security.

She went for a quick run in the park, came back, showered, and sat down at her computer.

A writer writes. A writer writes. A writer writes.

It helped to chant her new mantra as she ran. "Gorgeous female, financially independent, successful playwright, thirty—*er*—twenty…four, wishes to meet tall, handsome, young, and very rich non-smoking genius for indiscreet sensations leading to friendship, travel, casual relationship, serious relationship." Somewhere in there she remembered to breathe.

An early morning jog followed by five hours at the computer had become her routine five days a week for the past five months. She'd learned to time her outing with a guy, she'd seen in short shorts, whom she found very attractive. Up to now it had been a slight nod of recognition as they passed one another. Then a mumbled "Hi" and today it was an actual "G'morning." In movies, it was called the 'meet cute.' Things were looking up. Then it became a nod and a pointed finger in her direction. Definitely a friendly moving forward type greeting. She became bold and reversed her direction and started running alongside him asking if it was okay. He didn't object.

And that's how it went. That's how it went in the world of singles. She assumed he was single. No wedding ring. Her girlfriends told her it didn't mean a thing. Be careful. Your place or mine, good-looking? She hoped she hadn't said out loud what she was thinking. A wink, a nod, perhaps a verbal greeting, a wagging finger, a grunt. The unspoken second language in the world of single joggers. And she was part of it now.

If Ben could have his Carol thing, she could have her whatever his name was. Oh, that's right. Ben and Carol were on paper. A mere figment of her imagination. Sometimes she quoted lines not remembering if it was from one of her characters or from her. Was she psychic? Was there really a Carol in Ben's life? She didn't want to think about it. Easier to put it on paper. Fiction was the key to truth and ultimately to true happiness. A great line. A great thought. And all hers. One day, she'd have to use it in a play.

Reconstruct. Stop thinking about Ben.

Y ou're insatiable, Bernice," he barely got out for lack of breath.

"Brenda," she corrected him with gusto.

"Don't you need a coffee break? A cup of green tea?"

"You're so sexy."

"I'm not a machine."

"This is the real me," Brenda screamed.

Her park conquest. From upright positions to horizontal poses. There they were rolling around on her bed competing for the Gold Medal at the Olympics.

"The real me used to be Josh Roberts. I feel so weak I can't breathe."

"I'll breathe for both of us."

"Are you a widow?"

"Separated."

"A long time?"

"Almost six months. You?"

"Divorced."

"A long time?"

"Five years."

"Come on, Josh, let's do it."

"Not so fast. There are guys who died doing it."

"I don't believe you."

"That actor John somebody. Not a real person."

"John Garfield. I loved him. Remember that movie with Joan Crawford? He played the violin and she killed herself." Then Brenda cried out, "I WANT TO LIVE."

"I want to rest. God, what am I doing with this sex maniac I just met? Listen, I got nothing left. Do what you want. Just don't tell me." Josh went limp and laid back.

For a tiny moment, Brenda thought he was dead. Maybe it had been a little too quick. Maybe they should have talked first.

After a brief rest, during which she watched him lay there, they moved into the kitchen. He took over the tea making, and they sat and talked.

"So," she said, sipping her tea. "Good tea."

"Thanks."

"What now? Is this what it's going to be like?"

"What?"

"Being single I mean. Not…you know." She pointed first to herself and then to him.

The liquid refreshment having revived him somewhat, Josh opened up completely. "It isn't going to be easy. I gather I'm your first since? Just asking, not being nosy."

Brenda nodded. "You can tell, huh?"

He nodded. "You were together a long time?"

"Almost sixteen years."

"Kids?"

"Not even a canary."

"So I'm your first since the split."

"Uh-huh," Brenda mumbled.

"Then you're lucky it's me. Don't ask me why I know that. I just do. Because of the kind of guy I am. Maybe the reason you met me is because I can pass on what I know."

"How did you do it? How do you do it? Just asking. Not being nosy. Yes, I am."

He looked like he was trying to remember something.

"I hit a nerve," she said. "You don't have to say anything."

"No, it's okay. I don't mind. I was just trying to find the right way to say it without sounding preachy. Okay. Day two was my absolute worst. I went into the kitchen for breakfast like I always did. But I didn't have a clue. Instant coffee. I knew how to do that. I swear, I thought she was going to walk in any minute. I thought it was a bad dream. Are you sure you really want to hear all this? I mean, you've got your own baggage." He stopped talking.

Brenda could sense there was a determination in the way he related his story. It was pretty obvious he was over it. He wasn't bitter or angry or any of those emotions she still felt.

"Yes, I want to hear it. I'd love it from the man's point of view. I've talked to a few women, but they see it one way and men see it another way."

Brenda was attentive as he told her he'd married when they were nineteen. Had three kids right away. Was proud of them. He rattled off their ages. He loved them more than anything else. The perfect family so he thought. He stopped talking.

"So what happened?"

"One morning, we were at the kitchen table eating French toast with powdered sugar and cinnamon on top, just the way I like it. Out of the blue, she said she wanted out. No explanation, no reason, nothing. I still can't eat French toast."

"Just like that? I mean, what did she say?"

"Just like that. I want out. I don't want to be married anymore. Those were her exact words. I don't want to be married anymore."

"What about the kids?"

"As if they didn't exist. She took the Porsche and drove off. Didn't want anything else. We had just moved into this house in Westchester. I couldn't believe it. After about nine months, I finally believed it. I sold the house and moved into a big apartment in the city. Hired live-in help. Told the kids she was dead. Then I told them the truth."

"That had to be rough."

"Then it hit me. Any woman who leaves me isn't good enough. The hell with her, I said, and I meant it."

"What about the kids?"

"Therapy. Friends. Relatives. What's that saying? It takes a village."

"Wow. I guess I'm lucky. No kids, I mean. But then, our situation was different. We both agreed on the separation. No one just walked away."

"Then I went wild. Lots of women. I even took dance lessons. She always told me I was clumsy. I met lots of nice people, but I felt empty. I joined the kids in therapy, not always together you understand. I went once a week for two years. It helped to talk it out with a professional. Then about a year ago, a little over a year, I met a very nice woman, and we started seeing one other. She had a couple of kids. Twin boys. Then I realized something. I had my kids. I didn't want anyone else's. That's when I knew."

"Knew what?"

"I was ready to be by myself. That's when I started running and recently, I got into a Body Flow class. Kind of a combination of Tai Chi, pilates, yoga."

"That's quite a story. Thanks for sharing."

"What about you?"

They were silent for a second or two. She wasn't sure how much she wanted to say. Talking about Ben to another man, not to mention a stranger, made her feel disloyal. Then she let it all out.

"I was getting terrible backaches. Blamed it on sitting at the computer. The x-rays found nothing, but still the pain never went away. No one tied it up to my emotional state. The fact that my husband never touched me. Stopped touching me. The intimacy had totally gone. The struggle to look the other way, pretend it was just a glitch, caused even more pain. His mother blamed me for not having children because her son needed a son to complete him. Crap like that."

Josh was a good listener.

Brenda gently put her hand on his cheek. "I never did this before with anyone, Josh. I need you to believe that."

"Me neither," he replied.

"Really? You're so attractive," Brenda said.

"Never."

"I believe you. Do you believe me?"

"Yes," he said.

Brenda continued. "We stayed together pretending everything was okay. Actually, that's not true. We knew but we weren't ready to make the break. We'd had a good run. Fifteen, sixteen years. I want you to know I don't believe in divorce. It's terrible to say we had a good run. It's supposed to be forever, isn't it?"

"My therapist said it isn't sex that breaks up a relationship. It's dried up conversation."

"I believe that. Our dialogue had all but dwindled. I felt like I was encased in ice. An ice sculpture. A cold, hard, block of ice and the iceman didn't cometh. Eventually, we knew. He moved out. I stayed here. This," she gestured to the apartment, "is all mine."

"Great apartment. Great building. Great location. You can manage? Financially, I mean. It's a big place for one person. Beautiful in a prime location. Gotta be expensive."

"That's another story. He takes care of everything. Financially, I mean."

"Do you have a job?"

"I'm a dramatist. I'm also writing a novel. I can do that. Write two different genre pieces at the same time."

"Too lonely. You need people."

"I need to write."

"You need a job. If you don't need money, volunteer. You can still write."

It was out in the open now. Someone she could talk to about Ben. She could say his name out loud. She could talk about her feelings. You'd think it would be with women friends. But it hadn't happened that way. It sort of did, but not really. She always felt guarded with women contemporaries. Maybe men understood better. No underlying competition.

"Life was simple. Ben went to the office. Ben came home. We ate. We watched TV. We went to bed. On weekends, we saw our friends. We had money for anything we wanted. We were living the American Dream."

"The American Myth, you mean. It's never as simple as it seems."

"Will I ever sleep again? I sleep for four hours. Up for four. Down for four. I'm exhausted."

"Like marriage. A roller coaster. I went through that. You'll sleep again. Too soon to try for a relationship. You need to heal first. And you never know. You might like being single. You'll find out there's a whole life outside marriage. It won't be like it was before you were married, but it will be rewarding. You'll learn about yourself. Give it time."

They talked more in a couple of hours about real stuff than she and Ben had talked in a year. Josh said he learned. When he was married, he never talked. He thought his wife was supposed to know.

"Josh, what are you doing the rest of your life?"

"I can't save you, Brenda. No one can. Feel the pain. You'll get to know yourself. Be bold. Take a trip. A friend of mine just came back from Ireland. Loved it."

"Josh?"

"Yuh?"

"Would you mind holding me? Just holding me?"

He put his arms around her.

"I remember my father taking pictures of my mother. I was about five. She was all in white with a white gardenia in her black hair. I sniffed the gardenia and she yelled at me saying it would turn brown and die. I started to cry and my daddy picked me up and held me. Just held me until I stopped crying."

"Brenda, I can't hold you until you stop crying."

"Only for a little while."

And he did. For a little while. Just held her. And then he left. She cried a little. He must have changed his exercise time or route in the park because she never saw him again.

B ack at the computer, Brenda couldn't type fast enough. It was pouring out of her. She was considering changing the Brenda and Ben names.

                         (Brenda's phone rings. She
                         answers. It's Ben. Lights up
                         on split stage so they are
                         both visible to audience)

                         BEN

How many eggs do you use for an omelet?

                         BRENDA

Wait a minute. You are cooking?

                         BEN

Sometimes.

                         BRENDA

I guess I used four for us. So, now I guess

                         BEN

                         (Ignores her probe)

So I should figure two per person.

                    BRENDA

That's the best. Figure two per person. Don't
be afraid of the yolk. That's just hype. It's
the healthiest part.

                    BEN

Okay.

                    BRENDA

Okay. Ben?

                    BEN

Yuh?

                    BRENDA

If you prefer just egg whites, then about four
to six eggs. Egg whites, that is. It isn't too
much.

                    BEN

Okay, thanks.

                    BRENDA

You can buy egg whites so you don't have to do
that thing with the egg to get rid of the yolk.

                    BEN

Okay, thanks.

                    BRENDA

But if you prefer real eggs, you know how to

do that. Break the shell and pour it into each
side. Back and forth. That way, the white stays
and the yolk comes out.

                    BEN

Okay. Got it. Thanks, Brenda. I have to hang up
now. Thanks for the information.

                         (BEN clicks off. BRENDA just
                          stares into her phone)

And there it was. As she always said, why invent? All she had
to do was remember. It happened that Ben had just phoned
asking her how to make an omelet. She pulled up her play and
got it into the computer. Was this the beginning of a friendly divorce? They didn't seem to be letting go. He must have
been making the eggs for himself because if he had someone
there, that person would know most likely how to make eggs.

It had been a brief conversation, just about the eggs. She
needed to hear his voice again. They had just talked; yet, she
needed to talk to him. To hear him talk. There were no children, no dogs, no cats to keep them tied. It was just them.
She hit her speed dial with his number hating herself for
the conversation they were about to have. Would she ever
get him out of her system? How can you get over someone
who's still there? Maybe not living with you, but still there.

At first, the message came on, then he picked up much
to Brenda's relief.

"We tried, didn't we, Ben?"

After a slight pause, he said, "It wasn't an easy deci-
sion, Bren. You have to know that I never in a million years
thought it would end this way. We tried. Yes. I think we
tried, don't you? But sometimes, it doesn't always work out.
People grow apart sometimes. We have to move on, babe."

"Babe? You never called me babe."

"What?"

"Never mind. There's history, Ben. We have history. What do you do with the history?"

"Remember the good and let go of the bad, kiddo. It can be a struggle."

Now she was kiddo. Like a kid sister. "Too complicated. Life is too short to struggle, kiddo." If she was kiddo to him, he could be kiddo to her.

She couldn't stand this. What to do, what to do. Say what you mean, mean what you say, and don't say it mean. Where did she hear that before? Oh, her sister. One of the many AA pledges. She was going to have to take control of this conversation. He sounded a little out of it. Or maybe she was the one out of it. They went back and forth for a while. The longer they talked, the nastier it became. Why did she call him! Damn it. They went through the divorce every time they spoke to one another. It was exhausting. And yet she perpetuated it as much as he did.

"Death has got to be better than divorce," Brenda said quietly.

"Enough. I need a drink. You sound plastered. Probably won't remember any of this in the morning," Ben said. He clicked off.

"Ben? Ben? You don't hang up on me. I hang up on you."

Plastered? Sonofabitch. She hadn't had a drink in a couple of hours. He's the one who's probably drinking. Idiot! And with that, she took another sip of her wine before going back to her play.

B en's apartment was sparsely furnished. A strange turn of events for one of the top realtors in the city. He told himself he would get to it. But not today. He carried a plastic tray with plastic food from the kitchen to the living room. He sat down in a chair in front of the muted TV on the Nature channel, put the tray down on a small table, got up, went out to the kitchen, returned with a salt shaker. He salted his food. No one there now to tell him to watch his sodium intake. With that thought, he added more salt to the bland macaroni and cheese frozen dinner. Most nights he ate dinner out in a restaurant, but that was getting old since he ate lunch out every day. He started coming home after work and heating up a frozen dinner in the microwave. He turned the sound up on the TV and watched while he ate. A male voice was describing the scene of whales in the water.

"The male whale spots the female whale from a distance. In order to copulate successfully, the male whale needs a quarter of a mile run up. Pointing an erect organ of generation, which is six feet long, the male whale charges, miraculously scoring a direct hit into the female's private parts."

Ben changed the channel.

A female voice, British or Australian, he couldn't be sure,

was describing scorpions in a field. Ben wasn't that interested but he watched.

"The reproductive organs of the scorpion are simple. The external parts in both sexes are situated in the second segment beneath the forepart of the abdomen and consist of two small oval openings close together. Into each of these there opens in the male a curved, horn-lined sac with a lateral direction."

Ben became sad. Sadder than he'd ever been, not for the scorpions, but for his own non-existent sex life. He changed the channel.

"And the second program in our current series, Solo is Not So Low will deal with what to do if you have a heart attack. Tune in tomorrow evening at—"

"Jesus." Ben turned off the TV, got on his exercise bike, cycled like mad. Stopped. He rummaged around in a shoe box until he found it. The little black book he'd had for ages. Since high school. He looked through it, found a number, dialed, and waited for the greeting. It was a real person, not a voice message, which Ben half expected.

"Archie? Archie Sampler! How the hell are you? Been on any hayrides lately?" Ben let out a guffaw as he remembered the night.

The hayride was a hundred years ago when a bunch of pals went up to Connecticut for a weekend. Ben wasn't sure Archie was even with them, but he took a shot.

Archie said something on the other end. It sounded like "Ben who?"

"Ben Gordon. Looks like I'm the one who's single now. So that makes two of us. Thought we could get together."

Ben listened while Archie described his blissful domestic life.

"Oh, I see. I see. Well, good for you. Good for you. Long Island, huh? Finally settled down. Kept the same number."

Ben listened to more about the wonderful life of Archie Sampler.

"Three. Wow. And one on the way," Ben repeated, wondering why he didn't just hang up. That would be rude, so he listened while Archie continued to talk.

"Sure, sure, love to, Arch. I'm kind of tied up this week, but maybe next week. I'll give you a call." The conversation ended with Ben feeling worse than he had when he watched the scorpions on TV.

He thumbed through his book. Dialed several numbers without results. Looked up another number. "I don't think they're allowed to date if they're in a Convent." He tossed the book aside.

He turned on the TV again. A soap opera, judging from the expensive looking set, clothes, hair, and make-up. Everyone looked alike. He was glued to the snappy dialogue.

Her: "Don't lie to me. I know about you and that other woman."

Him: "What other woman? I never looked at another woman."

Her: "Don't lie to me."

Him: "It's true."

Ben: "I never looked at another woman. In sixteen years!"

Her: "Liar."

Ben: "Well, I looked. I didn't do anything."

Him: "Never."

Her: "Liar."

Ben: "Okay, okay, I did. Almost did. Once. But I didn't look."

A sound of a gunshot.

Ben fell to the floor. "You got me." Ben turned off the TV. "I'm okay, I'm okay. Divorce is not an ending. Divorce is a beginning. Thank God I've got money."

Without thinking much about it, he dialed his number. His old number. Now her number. Since the divorce wasn't final, technically still their number. Technically his number since he paid the bill.

She picked up on the first ring.

"Oh, it's you, Ben." Caller ID. Both a blessing and a curse.

"Hi. It's me, Ben. But you already know that."

"Can't talk. Up to my eyes in work. Creating like crazy. It's flying out of me. Go figure."

"Ben Gordon's residence. Mr. Gordon isn't in, but if you leave a message, he will return your call."

"Can it. You called me. What is it?" She was playing it tough but the truth was she was happy to hear from him. From anybody.

"Let's go out for a drink."

"No. Can't tonight." Maybe she should go. She already refused. Could she tell him she changed her mind? She was in her bathrobe. She'd have to dress and make-up.

"It's Saturday night, the loneliest night of the week."

"It's Thursday, luv." She'd just watched a British film and was drinking tea. Very impressionable was our Brenda.

"Love. The biggest, meanest four letter word there is."

"It means everything. It means nothing." What the hell. She could play the game for a while.

"My other half."

"So they say."

"Be nice. Without me, you wouldn't be able to live in that apartment. In Manhattan, the center of the world. Why are you being mean?"

"Because you take the life from me. I'm trying very hard to be a single person."

"I'm not stopping you," he said.

"It's easier for men."

"Not true. Women are much stronger. Women can be

alone much better than men. Men can't be alone. Women can be alone."

This wasn't going well. But she couldn't hang up on him. She actually felt sorry for him. Was she out of her mind? Did she want to see him? Maybe get back together? Did she? Whoa. All he asked was did she want to go out, not get remarried. He really wasn't such a bad guy, if you could get over the handkerchief number. And his mother. Maybe they made a mistake. Maybe they just needed a break. Ben was nice looking, financially well-off, generous. And in the months they'd been separated, she'd learned a thing or two about men. She'd read *Men are from Mars, Women are from Venus*; *The Road Less Traveled*; *Opening Our Hearts to Men*; and *God is a Matchmaker*. Not that she remembered a word of any of it. She watched Reality TV. She didn't remember any of that either, which said more of the content than her mind. And she pulled up a few life lessons on YouTube.

"It is my opinion, Ben, it's a miracle men and women get together at all, communication-wise. We exchange words, but do we really get it the way it was intended? So much goes into our own thoughts, how do we have space to take in anyone else's? If it wasn't for the sex, we'd kill each other. Oh, wait, we didn't, meaning the sex. We didn't have sex and we killed each other." She thought she might be delirious but couldn't stop her mouth. "Never mind what I'm saying. Just wipe it from your mind."

"Brenda? Is that you? Are you there?"

"Maybe. Maybe not." Where was this fool conversation going?

"I need to talk. Let's go out."

"On the phone."

"It's Saturday night. Date night."

"It's Thursday night. Okay, I'm going to say goodbye now."

"I get it. Someone's there, is that it?"

"It's not really any of your business."

"What's wrong, Brendie? You can tell Benny."

Brenda put the phone down and did a series of punches into the pillow in order to relieve the stress from this phone call. She took a deep breath and picked up again.

"When we were together, Ben, if you walked into the bedroom and I was lying in bed with a guy and we were naked, what would you have done?"

"What any gentleman would have done. I would have apologized for barging in and left the room."

"And therein lays the problem. It isn't supposed to be that way, dear heart. You should have challenged the interloper to a duel."

"My beautiful wife. My gorgeous, soon to be ex-wife."

"Why did we get married?" she asked suddenly. Did she really want to know? Or was she stalling, not wanting to let go of this bizarre connection with him.

"Everyone got married. I said I love you. You said I love you, too. I said will you marry me. You said yes. So we did. We said it would be forever. We were in Mexico. We were walking up that hill. You were sweating like a pig. Your eye make-up was running down your face. Your hair was all matted and flat against your head. I asked myself is that what I want to look at the rest of my life."

"What was your answer?" She hadn't even thought about that until now. And he remembered the details. Her make-up running down her face. Her hair. This was not the Ben she had come to know in the past few years.

"You know the answer."

"Anyway, it wasn't in Mexico. It was at that restaurant in Boston. We'd gone to Cape Cod for the weekend." Was she getting flirty?

"The first time. And you said something like ask me every day and one day I'll say yes. The second time was in

Mexico. Don't you remember? It was very romantic."

"And how did that go for you?" Now sarcasm.

"What do you mean? It was romantic."

She'd had enough. "I'm saying goodnight now, Ben, and you should follow suit."

"We're not playing cards. You're really quite a nasty piece of work. My mother was right. Boy, are we doing the right thing."

"You are causing me pain. I'm hanging up." If he calls again, I won't answer. The up and down of the conversation had made her very nervous. What was going on?

She pulled up the novel and hit the keys like a mad woman, talking aloud as she wrote.

"*SEX UNZIPPED*. Chapter Two Hundred. Is There Life After Death? Maxine danced like the music was made just for her. She became the music. When she danced she was young and happy and safe. When she danced she didn't feel abandoned. When she danced, she forgot that she hadn't heard from Valentino in six months. The louse."

Brenda stopped writing. She was crying. Not about Maxine. Not about Valentino. Why couldn't her life go right? What was it about the Glimcher sisters that couldn't stay married to a guy and in Eve's case, got married again and again and again. Will that be her fate, too? Will there be another marriage? Will she give up men? Become celibate? Will she have affairs one after the other? Is it the idea of being alone that frightened her?

She dried her eyes and moved on to the play. She made notes. What she hadn't figured out yet was the ending. The characters were in between, but maybe that wasn't the major thread. She didn't know yet. Do the Jordans get back together at the end? Or is it too late? They go their separate ways. Friends. Not friends. He meets someone. She meets someone. They go out on dates with one another. It can't continue. It does continue. She becomes a lesbian. He's gay. Always suspected, but only now could come out.

Writing was easy. The decisions were hard. Keep calm and write on.

As for Ben, he wasn't stupid. He knew the score. It wasn't about sex or about money. About anything really. He longed for someone to touch. To touch him. Just a touch. Sitting on the couch side by side watching a television show or a movie and putting your hand on her shoulder, her arm, her thigh, her hand. Just a touch. Hearing a friend had died and phoning to tell her. Discovering a new mole on your shoulder and asking her to look. Was it multi-colored? Oddly shaped? Were there any others like it on his body? Ringing her just before leaving the office to go home. What's for dinner? Should I bring anything? Do you want to eat out? I got theatre tickets for a new show on Saturday. A pair. Two seats together. One is a lonely number. Where's my blue shirt? All the wheres, whats, whens, hows. With someone there to answer. Freedom had its price. It was too high a price. Even for a rich man, it was too high.

Divorce never begins on the day of the actual split. It begins way before and festers until it explodes. Terrorism never begins on the day it happens. A strange analogy: divorce and terrorism.

How absolutely fitting that on the day of her final decree, Brenda finished the play about the Jordans with the working title of *In Between*. She had two endings. One, the two characters get back together; and two, they go their separate ways. She still wasn't sure about the ending, but it was time to let it go. Often, a playwright will hang on to something, rewriting and rewriting, never finishing it, just because the fear of rejection is stronger than the belief in success. She made a hard copy and packed it up and sent it off to the artistic director at Stageworks/Hudson, a regional theatre upstate New York with a solid reputation for accepting new plays without going through an agent. What appealed to her was the fact that it was a relatively small theatre with a seating capacity of one hundred, it was in New York, albeit not Broadway, but the fact remained they were dedicated to bringing adventurous theatre productions and programs of high artistic quality to the City of Hudson, Columbia County, and the greater Hudson Valley.

She looked at the piece of paper that dissolved the marriage. Just like that.

A piece of paper.

She called Ben, not sure why, but who else was going through the same thing she was going through at the same time.

He picked up on the first ring. "This is Ben."

"I know. Hi."

There was a slight pause, neither of them sure if they should be mad or what or what was the correct procedure in a friendly divorce, if indeed this was that. And who makes the first move. Well, she had made the move by calling him. After the brief hellos and how are yous and all that crap that means nothing and then finally the bit about did you get the piece of paper about you know what, he said something profound.

Sort of profound.

Know what I'm gonna miss most?"

"Can't imagine."

"Your banana fritters."

"And least?" Brenda asked. That was one dish she did do pretty well. Eggs were easy.

"Your cauliflower fritters."

"That never did come out right, did it?"

"So?" he said. "What's going on?"

"So," she said. And then the words poured out of her mouth before she even knew what she was saying. "Would you like to come over?" Once out, impossible to take back. She didn't want to take them back. She meant it.

"Yes." That's all he said.

No goodbyes were necessary.

She showered, slipped on a pair of jeans and a cute little top and went into the kitchen. She checked that all the ingredients were in house and started the preparation for the banana fritters.

Ben arrived in under an hour.

They went into each other's arms.

They held each other a second without words. An entanglement of friendship, tenderness, love, forgiveness, regret, relief, and a little of that old thing, hate.

"I wish the marriage had been as exciting as the divorce," she quipped.

"I wish you'd been as attractive then as you are now."

"Have we made a mistake?"

If he did hear her, he didn't answer. He was long gone into the entrance to that ecstasy place as if it was a new skin next to him. She stopped the chatter. She felt what he felt.

They made love like it was their first time. After, she made him the banana fritters. In the nude.

"I don't know anyone else who cooks naked," he said admiring her body. "You look good. You always had a good body."

After the after, they made love again. Then they put on their clothes and after the after after, they talked.

"Is this weird or what?" he said.

"I can't promise monogamy, you know. I've been on my own over a year. Do we date one another or what?"

"It's the same for me. You know how that is. For a man, I mean." He pulled out a white handkerchief from his pants pocket and blew his nose.

And that's when she knew the answer. Despite the great sex all of a sudden, and it was, she couldn't forget that this was Ben. She didn't divorce him to see more of him. "I think we can look at this as a one night stand." It had been a lusty thrust and that's all. "We were both just a little horny and familiarity does have benefits."

"Crazy, isn't it? Do you think other divorced couples do this?" Ben asked.

"How should I know? Maybe it works for some. I don't know. You know, Ben, since we're being so honest, I never thought I'd like being single. You were right. I actually like it. I think."

"Will you take back your maiden name?"

"I thought about it. But no. I'm still Mrs. Gordon, in name only of course. Professionally, it has a nice ring to it. I'll drop the Mrs."

"Brenda Gordon. It does have a nice ring to it. And it looks good in print."

"Are you seeing anyone now?" she dared to ask. And it felt all right. She wasn't jealous or bitchy. Maybe she wanted him to ask her about her love life.

"Early stages. You? I heard you've been seen around with an Asian guy. A big entrepreneur. Good looking. I must admit, I was a little surprised."

"Just a few dates. Nothing else. Subject closed."

"Mine's young. In fact, much younger. We'll see. She's

moved in. We'll be moving into a bigger apartment together. Maybe. I don't want to rush it."

"I guess we just wish each other luck and move on. I'm glad it isn't weird between us, Ben. It isn't, is it? Weird, I mean. I think maybe we're just better as friends than husband and wife. Friends with benefits, I think is the expression."

I dea for new play titled, *An Ideal Marriage*. Very British, very Noel Coward.

Until death us do part. For death, read life. Until life us do part. Around three pm Friday, wife starts to think about a lover, possibly husband, maybe not. Monday to Thursday, she's got other things to think about. Husband arrives home at half past six Friday and departs by ten Monday morning. A very strong alternative would be just after lunch on Sunday. An early lunch. One meal during the weekend is to be prepared by the husband and breakfast is always prepared by him and brought to her in bed without her asking, although it is clear she didn't marry him for his culinary prowess. If she wants intellect, she can go to the library. One meal to be eaten out in a restaurant. Regarding special occasions such as birthdays and anniversaries: Should they fall between Monday and Thursday, they are to be celebrated between Friday and Monday. Christmas is a possible exception. Hopefully, it will not be necessary to communicate by telephone between Monday and Thursday. He is not to bring home dirty laundry. Other arrangements must be made. Some dame he might meet casually in between Monday and Thursday could do the washing and ironing. Exception: If they employ a maid, he can bring home his laundry, but he is not to screw the maid. In any case, she will be old and ugly. And last, but by no means least, he is not to bring home a sexually transmitted disease, no matter how old and ugly.

The theatre in Hudson gave her positive feedback on the play, but couldn't offer a contract. They liked the premise, but said it still needed work. They liked her writing and wanted to see something else she'd written. Not great news, but not bad either. She was on a roll. Maybe her notes on the ideal marriage could be developed as a one-woman show. Maybe. She liked the idea of a two-hander. Here was proof she didn't always need a man to be happy. She had a life. And she had more than just the possibility of a production to look forward to pending a new draft. It didn't seem so important right now. Why? She'd met someone on the train from Hudson back to the city. Someone she really liked and wanted to get to know. This single existence was kind of fun. She could flirt with all and sundry.

Tom Winslet wasn't 'sundry' by any stretch of the imagination. He was a writer on the threshold of a major career as it appeared. Two screenplays, three plays. She looked him up online. They became an item. He wrote. She wrote. There was a kind of distance between them that she liked. She felt less needy. And he was independent. This was good. She was growing. She liked to say that they were in like. It felt healthy. They made plans for the future.

One afternoon, her doorbell rang.

It seemed odd because of the time of day. Not that her doorbell hadn't ever rung but this time, her premonition had been right. It was odd. There was Ben standing in the doorway with his briefcase in one hand and his other hand clutching the handle of a suitcase on wheels.

"Ben!" She hoped that wasn't his dirty laundry in the suitcase.

"Are you alone? I did ring the bell."

"Yes, I heard it. Yes, I'm alone. You look terrible. Are you sick?"

He walked past her into the living room and sat down. "I feel terrible." And he went on to tell his ex-wife about the problems with his current girlfriend, although given the current circumstances, his soon to be ex-girlfriend.

"Let me understand this, Ben. You want my advice about your girlfriend?"

"Ex."

"But you said she's hasn't moved out."

"That's why I'm here. Believe me, a stretch in the clink would be more appealing."

"Ask her to move out. No, don't ask. Tell her."

"Not as easy as it sounds."

"Why not?"

"Because half the music population in the world has taken up residence until they get the prose opera, whatever the hell that is, that they're working on finished."

"I thought you had a studio apartment."

"She doesn't have any place to go. None of them appear to have any place to go." Ben got up and fixed himself a drink, holding out the glass to her.

"No thanks, but help yourself. Well, what are you going to do?"

"It's like spaghetti junction over there with all the wires and cables. What the hell am I going to do?"

"That was my question. Does she think you went home to your mother? You don't have a dog to walk, so that excuse is out. Let's see. Door to door salesman. Are there still Fuller Brush men? Okay, so what did you tell her?"

"I didn't tell her anything. I sneaked out and left a note in the fridge about some urgent business in Florida. Urgent family business."

"What kind of urgent family business."

"Your death."

"That's urgent. Ben, seriously, what are you going to do? You could go to a hotel. You really could go to Florida."

"Not a bad idea. I need a tan. I'm known for my suntans. Why don't you fly down with me? It's okay now between us. We'll have a good time."

"We can't do that."

"Oh, I see what you mean. We won't go to Key West. It wouldn't matter. They've probably had a million double attempted jumps from the roof of the hotel since then. We can go to Miami. They don't know us."

"Not a good idea, Ben. That was another major catastrophe. What is it with us and roof tops?"

They had been fighting like cats and dogs, and she ran up to the roof to get away from him. He had followed and they struggled. It didn't look good if anyone was watching and everyone was watching. They were asked to leave the hotel.

"If you remember," she continued, "I vowed never to return to Florida again. But there's another reason I can't go with you to Florida."

Ben wasn't listening. "I know. I'll stay here until she moves out. That's a better idea. On the sofa bed in the den. It's a good thing I never took it. It's perfect. I'll be gone all day. You won't even know I'm here."

"Ben, listen, I've met someone. It could be serious. I

think it is. We are discussing moving to London for a year." She paused. "He's a writer."

In Ben's usual insensitive persona, he thought that was a perfect solution. While Brenda was gone, he would move back into the apartment and give notice on his rental. After all, they weren't going to give up an apartment on Central Park that they happened to own. Technically, that he owned.

"Well, Brenda, good for you. Let's drink on it. Oh, you're not drinking. I'll make some coffee." He headed for the kitchen.

Was it such an outlandish notion? The idea of him moving in. "Stick to the instant," she called after him."

"I know how to percolate now."

"That's what you told me the other time."

"I wish you didn't have such a good memory."

"Memory is my business. That's why writers suffer. We have to remember what everyone spends their lives trying to forget."

"That was funny."

"It wasn't meant to be."

"No. I mean about percolating the tea leaves thinking it was coffee."

"And me drinking it because I didn't want to hurt your feelings."

"We'd only been married a few months."

"A hundred years ago. Somehow the taste of percolated tea remains forever."

"It never leaves you."

And with that choice bit of banter, albeit nothing new, Ben disappeared into the kitchen, leaving Brenda really wondering about these new relationships she was entering into with both the ex-husband and the new boyfriend. It wouldn't be so bad. Ben would be here. It was evident that his girlfriend would leave, probably with one of the musicians, leaving a note stuck in between his thousand handkerchiefs. Life was truly like a book. You never knew what was next until you turned the page. While Ben would be looking after the property, she and Tom would be three thousand miles away in fabulous London. A new chapter was about to begin. It was a relief to know and accept that she was a better ex-wife than a wife. What Ben thought or believed was to do with Ben, not with her.

Tom was her escape. Was that really it? Did she trust him? There was that little voice in her head that said he was a womanizer; that she'd never come before his work. Or other women. He was matinée idol handsome and he knew it. A chick magnet. And women were attracted to writers. Hadn't she been attracted to him? Knowing something and doing something about it are two different things. She needed to risk it. She needed to get out of New York, away from Ben, away from the apartment, and into new surroundings.

*T*om *is an evolved individual. He totally accepts and understands the relationship I have with Ben without jealousy. That's a joke. What relationship? Tom is working on a new play and busy making all the arrangements for London. I'll just have to trust as I haven't seen any evidence of it. He tells me all I have to do is show up. I think he's the man I'm going to marry. Yes, dear journal, I still believe in marriage, despite my ravings. I think it would be totally neat to have two writers together. Not that I want to collaborate with him. No. He'd do his thing; I'd do my thing. There would be an understanding of two artists. Meanwhile, I'm back with the play and the fictional Jordans. The first draft as I've always said is verbal diarrhea. Subsequent drafts are the sculpting, where the chisel goes to work. First, the heart, then the head. Right now, I'm in between heart and head.*

A writer writes.

After six hours, she had completed only four pages of something. Maybe just drivel. She didn't care. She was writing. A monologue for Brenda Jordan, not really sure where it would fit or if it would work at all. It made her laugh when she read it aloud, but she wasn't sure it would work in the long run. Main thing was to get it down on paper and look at it later. As every writer knows, it is easier to cut than to add. The theatre had said they wanted it zippier and funnier.

Tragedy was easy. Comedy is hard.

                    BRENDA

                    (Reading aloud from her di-
                    ary)

                    AN AFFAIR TO FORGET.

Monday the 15th. New York.

8 a.m. Woke up. Checked it off list. Went out to the kitchen. Had a mug of instant decaffeinated coffee with coconut milk creamer and a heaping hunk of cottage cheese and cherry jam on the edge of a knife.

8:25 - Threw up.
Wednesday the 17th. Los Angeles.

8 a.m. Woke up. Threw up.
Called Peter in London. He said Terry and Kevin called Paul in New York from Paris to get her number in Los Angeles.
Terry called from Paris. Peter called from London two hours later. He had to go to Geneva. I went to the gym to do a yoga class. Terry called again and left a message on my voice mail telling me to call Pip in Brussels. I called Larry in New Hampshire to get Pip's number, got mis-routed to a Lilah in New Mexico, left a message for Eddie on voice mail in Honolulu. Went to Elizabeth Arden's for a facial, ate a

turkey sandwich on whole wheat with lettuce and tomato, a complimentary lunch for the customers, went back to the hotel and got the big news by phone. The doctor was wrong. I am pregnant.

PART II

The whole world was crammed into London's square mile. It turned out that Tom hadn't organized a damn thing. This character flaw surprised her since he had told her he was taking care of the arrangements. They were in a pickle. There were no vacant flats or hotels in their budget. It was a nightmare. For her, not him. He seemed oblivious. All that mattered to him was he was in London. She hadn't arrived at that great declaration yet. Tom looked up an old friend from New York who had moved to London years ago and thankfully, he managed to find them a room—*room* being the operative word—in an area that reminded her of all the places she had never wanted to be. It was a kind of boarding house in not the best part of London.

As they were climbing the stairs to their room on the fourth floor, they passed the bathroom on the third floor. She quickly learned the bathroom was the name of the room where you took a bath. The toilet was called the loo, not a john, although frequently referred to as the toilet in order to distinguish it from the bath. Their room consisted of twin beds, cots really, a kitchenette against a wall, and the ever present smell of damp. Tom said it was a temporary situation, so they could do it. They were in London! They more or less were going to have to live out of their suitcases strewn across the floor as there wasn't enough space to un-pack everything. And that's how they started their new life. Tom thought it was great.

Brenda didn't share his enthusiasm. She was crazed. She could leave; check into a good hotel; go home. What was holding her here? Was Tom still that romantic figure she knew in New York? Where had he gone? Where was Ben when she needed him? Tom equaled chaos. But she was be-sotted by him. He didn't seem to have a worry nerve. Ben equaled fastidiousness even though she loathed it most of the time.

Five days into this nightmare, Tom was off to a place he heard writers hang out. Wasn't she a writer? Why wasn't she invited? Best he scoped it out first he told her. She'd had it. She was going to do something about where they were going to live even if he hadn't and wasn't going to. She didn't care if she was coming across as the gum chewing ugly American. Off she sped around the corner to the underground station where there was a newsagent shop and a notice board. Too impatient to write down her request on the white index card provided by the shop for advertising, this American prin-cess needed immediate gratification. Putting out an SOS on the Internet would take too long and would be too involved. Besides, she wasn't savvy enough technical-wise.

Her way was to stand there and publicly announce at the top of her lungs: "Would anyone like a room with two beds, kitchenette, and separate bathroom around the corner?"

The way it came out, it sounded like the bathroom was literally around the corner from the flat, but she didn't care. And judging from the mob that instantly surrounded her, no one else cared either. Before she finished the sentence, she was surrounded by dozens of people desperately look-ing for accommodation. A quick look into the crowd and Brenda decided on the couple with the baby.

"Follow me," she gestured and led the Spanish couple, who spoke acceptable English, to the house. The couple said they must have the place at any cost. They'd been up for two nights. She didn't think she needed to mention she and Tom had signed a year lease. Actually, she hadn't signed anything. She thought it was a month to month deal until Tom explained it was a year lease.

The housekeeper, who was responsible for servicing and letting the flatlets, lived in the basement of the building. The housekeeper hesitated. It was highly irregular this type of thing and she didn't like having to change the sheets before the weekly regime. And besides there was a lease to deal with. Brenda was very convincing. She slipped the house-keeper fifty pounds and paid the first month's rent for the new tenants. Money talked in any language.

After packing up their stuff, Brenda dragged it all down to the street, sat on a suitcase, and waited for Tom to return. They were now officially homeless. When Tom returned, she quickly explained what had happened.

"Jesus, Brenda. Okay, I'll make a few phone calls."

Fortunately, a Brit he knew from college was leaving for the South of France that very minute and offered his mews house in Chelsea for a fortnight. Included in the deal were a daily maid and a cat. Surely, in two weeks, they'd find a permanent place to live.

"Well that was lucky," was all Brenda could offer.

"See? You never have to worry with me. I'll always get us straight."

The cat named Lennon (after, you guessed it, John Lennon) hated Brenda on sight. It was mutual. The daily maid known simply as Mrs. P. or T., Brenda never got it, would arrive around eight in the morning, bring the temporary occupants, still in bed, a pot of tea and toast with orange marmalade. She washed the dishes from the night before, lightly dusted, smoked a cigarette, drank a cup of tea, ironed whatever needed ironing, smoked another cigarette, cleaned the kitchen and the bathroom, took care of the cat's needs, and took her leave.

Brenda and Tom took advantage of the break from household woes and resumed their lovemaking. He was the Tom who Brenda knew in New York. They walked everywhere, went to museums, and went to the theatre every night. And then reality set in once again. They really had to find a place to live. It wasn't until the day before their absentee host was due back from his holiday that Brenda, once again, had to take charge. Through another bulletin board at another underground station, Brenda found them the perfect place to live, the only drawback being that the one bedroom flat faced north which meant it would be cold and dark. It was August. No matter. They were told they had missed the two days of summer in June. None of it mattered. By the time winter rolled around, they would have got used to it.

Surprisingly, the fact that Tom had said he would take care of everything and did nothing was actually okay with her. She decided not to make an issue of it. It wasn't his thing. So what. It made her a little more independent. She didn't have to rely on a man. It gave her confidence. A twisted way of looking at it, she knew, but maybe not. She was in a good relationship with a man she loved. And he loved her. Ben wore suits; Tom wore jeans and boots. It was a big turn on. They were in their new home with a one-year lease and an option to renew. In London! What could possibly go wrong?

22

I t was not an elaborate ceremony as in all those pie in the sky bridal magazine descriptions. It was…what's the word? Different. Even bizarre. And also at the same time, kind of romantic, given the location. They had discussed it. Why not? He had never been married. No baggage. She was divorced. No children. Her baggage was three thousand miles away. So, on a Monday morning in January at eleven at the famed Chelsea Town Hall in London, the groom, wearing a black shirt and black pants and maroon cowboy boots; the bride, wearing a long sleeve purple knee-length silk dress, black tights, and red high-heeled boots with extremely dangerous pointed toes, waited to be wed along with several other couples, all grinning in a way that displayed a collective mental age of three. In attendance were Tom's college mate and their London neighbor, Baig Osman, a former Indian ambassador to somewhere.

While waiting for their turn to be hitched, the groom disappeared out the side door. Uh oh. As it turned out, it was for a smoke. He didn't smoke. Boy, was he nervous. And she wasn't doing too well, either. It must have been a foot long cigarette. Had he done a flit? It should only take ten minutes. That's how the ten minute break in a business meeting came about. Someone figured out somewhere that it took ten minutes to finish a cigarette, so that's how it became known as the ten minute break which everyone knows lasts twenty minutes.

Not sure if the groom was a runaway, Baig assured her that she would get married as that's why he was there. For insurance. Even at seventy-nine he was quite appealing. So she must have had some thought that the groom had fled because she was weighing up Baig's words the way you do real quick in your head. But he couldn't have offered her years ahead with lots of words yet to be written as her Tom. He did, however, own his flat which was considerably larger and much nicer than her one-bedroom. She was sure he hadn't had sex in at least fifteen years. Well, she wasn't sure, but you kind of can figure these things out about a man who lived alone, didn't seem to have women friends, stayed in mostly. All that kind of thing. But, the big but, it would mean permanent residence in London. Maybe not a bad thing. She'd move into a well-appointed flat with a man who might die sooner than her; who wouldn't leave for another woman or go out for a ten minute smoke break when he didn't smoke. And on occasion, at her or their disposal would be a chauffeur-driven Jaguar. Midnight blue. That summed up Ambassador and Mrs. Baig Osman. She had to remember this scenario. It was a terrific story.

The Ambassador and the Writer. Intriguing. When East Meets West. Boring.

Tom reappeared reeking of tobacco. Proof he really had been smoking. She pretended it didn't bother her. The smoke. She stifled her gagging. Boy, was he nervous. Suddenly she didn't care. She had back-up.

Go, her little inner voice said. He isn't the marrying kind. Oh, what the hell, we're here. It'll be okay. It'll be fun. Think of his voice. You love his voice. And remember what you were attracted to when you first saw him in New York.

Love at first sight. That first attraction. The 'meet cute,' like in a film. He's adorable in his boots and cowboy hat.

She didn't listen to her inner voice. When the hope of everlasting love appears in your front yard, does anyone listen to their inner voice?

Brenda Martha Glimcher Gordon Winslet. BMGGW. Quite a mouthful. She was determined to keep writing as Brenda Gordon. Here she was in marriage number two. Still a writer. Still her. But who her? Which her? Had she married too soon after her divorce? Did she really know Tom? Why was she having these doubts? A little late for that, don't you think, Brenda? She believed him when he said he loved her. She even believed her when she said she loved him. She had hoped for a lover, boyfriend, best friend, as well as husband. Silly. Where did she ever get that notion? The movies. There was no guarantee that two writers wedded to each other make for a good recipe. No guarantees about anything. She hadn't thought it through but she didn't care. It would be a kind of on the job training, as it were. You're never too old to grow up. She was Mrs. Winslet. And Mr. Winslet smelled delicious.

The cruelest reminder of who she was came during a candlelit dinner designed to seduce her lover, boyfriend, best friend—still wishful thinking. They were having dinner at home. Vanilla scented candles. The whole bit. The music was romantic. Ballads on the CD player by Barbra Streisand—his favorite.

She, Brenda, not Barbra, had slaved over roast beef and

Yorkshire pudding. When he finished his meal, just like that, he got up from the dining table without so much as a glance in her direction. Not one compliment on her efforts. Nothing. He pulled his chair away from the table, didn't put the chair back to the table, and headed for his desk on the other side of the room. Back to his mistress. The living room was his writing domain; hers was the bedroom. Actually, they had flipped a coin when they moved in and that's how it came out.

"You're leaving me? Just like that?" She indicated the table arrangement with a limp wrist. Table arrangement, of course, included her.

Acting as if he didn't know what she meant, a 'huh,' implied by the look, said it all. And then as an afterthought like maybe he knew he was doing something wrong, he said, "I'm right here in the same room." Then the guilt. "For chrissakes, Brenda," he said coarsely. "Grow up."

Brenda. A bumpy road ahead. Usually, it was Bren. Sometimes honey. "It's supposed to be a romantic evening," she kind of whimpered. "Candles. Roast beef. Yorkshire pudding. From scratch. I worked hard for tonight. You can't just get up and leave the table."

"Can't? I can and I did. Come on, babe, you know I'm in the middle of a script."

Now it's babe. "You don't give a shit about my feelings."

"Where is this coming from?"

"Well, I thought tonight would be for us. It's been a long time." To her, a week was a long time. She hadn't really been counting. Not exactly.

"You know how I am when I'm in the zone."

The zone argument. How do you come back from that? "It's lonely sometimes."

No reply.

"Tom?"

"It wouldn't be if you would do your own work."

"It isn't coming. I'm empty. Tonight, tonight, I need you tonight." She went over to him and put her arms around his neck, her lips reaching for his mouth. That beautiful sexy mouth. Not for her now. That beautiful sexy mouth was zipped tight now.

He moved her arms off him, not that gently, and standing up facing her, blurted out, "Do you want to be known as a writer or a fucker?"

Pow! Like an uppercut jab across your kiss-waiting, kiss-willing, kiss-hoping cheek. Did he mean the sting to sting so much? It was a few seconds before she could come back with a reply.

"Why not both?" she mumbled, not hearing herself.

"Because one or the other gets watered down. Both, actually," he answered, sitting down at his desk as if nothing had just happened. Seconds and he was back with his manuscript. She had become invisible.

And that was that. She could recognize an end of scene cue. She returned to the dinner table solo unable to finish her meal. Thanks to the wine she guzzled, she was able to clear the table and get into the kitchen. The kitchen. The little woman's place in the home. Did she secretly harbor that notion? Did he think that? Was anyone thinking at all?

There they were, holed up, former sex slaves, because at one time it was hot, now sexually marooned in that so-called intellectual prison of writing. Sex Slaves. The writer in her wanted to remember that phrase for something. A title. A theme. In the midst of the slap, there it was. Somehow she was still alive.

As a boyfriend, Tom had offered fun most of the time and lots of laughs. Was it that piece of paper that diluted the passion? In such a brief time? One in two gets divorced. The institution of marriage. Thinking back, was there ever real passion, the right kind of passion? That need you, want you, love you more than life itself, I would die for you kind of passion. The answer, when she could bear to face it, was a big fat no. She'd been caught up in his perfect straight nose, blue-gray eyes, dark wavy hair, cleft chin, slim body. And the sound of his voice. His voice alone was worth the price of admission. He was the polar opposite of Ben. Ben was a businessman. Tom was a creative artist. Like her. Wasn't that the best deal? That they were both writers? Shouldn't it work?

She knew all of it, all the pros and cons, but stuffed it all down somewhere because the bottom line, when she could be honest with herself, was that she didn't want to be alone. That was it. She'd been out there for a little while and didn't want to be out there anymore. She wanted to be in love; to believe she was in love. And the fact that, and this was major, that they were planning to take off and go and live in London for a year. That they could. That they were both free to take off like that, not just for a ten day holiday, but to live. She loved the idea that she had found another writer who had the freedom to move around the world. Why didn't she have the foresight to realize that this same kind of flexibility meant he could move on. Move on, that is, away from her. Moving guy. But it wasn't going to happen. Not to her. That kind of thing happened to other women. Not to her. She was too smart for that. Guys didn't dump her. She was the dumper, not the dumpee.

Looking back, her instincts hadn't been so bad. She'd had bad dreams. She'd had premonitions. Those gut feelings one tends to ignore. Run, her head said. Run fast and don't look back. Stay, her heart said. It will be all right. What do hearts know!

Two single people arriving in London town; happy and carefree. Looking forward to the new adventure. One year in London in a modestly furnished flat in Chelsea. But why not stay single? Why marriage? Because she thought it would hold him. That's why. Forever. That's how dumb she was. Dumb. Dumb. Dumb.

Boy marries girl. No. Girl marries boy. What a laugh. Or as the Brits would say, what a bloody balls up.

Miraculously, they actually stayed together until the London sojourn ended. Together should be read loosely. Sex was an occasional event. It was good, but never enough for her. He thought twice a week was excessive. Was he a closet queen? He did attend a lot of writers' events. Men only, he told her. She believed him, but not really. She never cooked for him again. Except to discuss the divorce, few words were uttered. He was deep into his writing. She remained blocked and went to a lot of plays, telling herself not to feel guilty because her brain was at the 'taking in' stage. A novelist reads a lot of novels; a playwright sees a lot of plays. So she was, in a manner of speaking, working.

The year passed, the lease was up, and they had to divide what stuff had accumulated in a semi-furnished flat. Is this yours? That's mine. Remember the day we bought that? Hadn't she gone through that with Ben? They ended up giving away most of the stuff.

Back in New York, it was time to take stock. Two marriages, two divorces. What the hell was wrong with her? Ben had moved out of the apartment. It was time to pull herself together. Hard to swallow, but she heard Tom moved back to London into some posh Mayfair flat with a woman of a certain age who loved young writers. To crown it, she was Lady something or other. How Tom met her she'd never know. She was sure it wasn't on the Piccadilly line on the tube. How could she have been so blind? Younger man, older woman. Maybe he really was gay. You never know how you're going to react at the end of a relationship. She always imagined she'd lie on her sofa for a year listening to self-help tapes. It didn't happen that way. She went the other way, believing those who said the quickest way to get over someone is in the arms of someone else.

While the ink was drying on her divorce papers, she was seeing Peter, this man whose wife had recently walked out on him. A well-planned getaway, Brenda thought, on the wife's part, because all she left in the house was the kitchen table. How did Peter and she meet? Through her second husband. The four of them had often gone out together. She happened to see Peter's letter to the editor in a local newspaper responding to some environmental piece and called to congratulate him. He invited her to lunch. Innocent enough. She told him her news; he told her his news.

Their mutual splits turned his aforementioned lunch invitation into: "Oh, in that case, let's have dinner." And that's how it began.

He was tall and lean and utterly vain about his good looks: blue eyes, chiseled cheekbones, full mouth, thick shiny silver hair. He fell into the category of one of those Brits who had fallen in love with America, having come over for work, and stayed. She was a sucker for a British accent. She liked Peter. She thought he liked her. He was, in a manner of speaking, a more mature gentleman, and was obviously hurting that his much younger wife had left him. It was easier to focus on his woes and soothe his wounds than deal with her own. Rebound was not in her dictionary, so she plunged in, siding with him for having been left, poor thing.

She ignored all the obvious signs that they weren't exclusive. She would peak at greeting cards around his house. One of those brownstones on the upper West Side. The cards were signed by Judi or Pat or Cindy with handwritten expressions of how much they had enjoyed their evening. Was Brenda angry with him? Of course not. She blamed herself for snooping. Just women friends, she told herself. Didn't she have men friends?

Meanwhile, her writing was suffering. Non-existent would be a more apt description. She'd sit down, try, but couldn't focus. The relationship, for lack of a better word, went on for about seven months. He knew how to navigate, maybe not the right word, but it would do, around the bedroom. After a long drought in her marital bed, in both marriages, she thought she'd found her perfect match. All she wanted, she told herself, was regular sex with a regular guy. Peter fit the profile.

She loved his house. Nearly two thousand square feet and well-appointed. It was where they hosted parties together. His friends, her friends, never their friends. This was a whole new role for her. While he did the shopping, prepping, and cooking, she was the master of presentation. It was an opportunity for her to show off her creativity with food as long as she didn't have to prepare it. Throwing herself into what she imagined was domestic bliss, she loved all of it.

This must be what a really good marriage is like. Every day like this.

One Saturday night, she cooked dinner for them at her place. Just her way of reciprocating for the many dinners he'd cooked and the many restaurants he had taken her to. Not exactly cooked. She bought a ready-made chicken. But she did do the salad from scratch. She was good at salads. Soft lights, candles, and music set a romantic mood. A brief reminder of that other romantic setting with ex-husband Tom, the image which she quickly erased from her brain.

Peter looked across the dining table at her looking at him and said softly, "I'm feeling romantic, darling."

You have to imagine that with an English accent. Someone from, say, Alabama just couldn't pull it off. She took a sip of her dry white wine, eyes never coming off his, and smiled. All part of the dance. He stood up and took her hand in his. She told him to snuff out the candles while she turned out the lights. The temperature dropped quickly and reminded them both that after a certain age practicality becomes more important than the heat of the moment. Lights get turned out, candles get snuffed out, clothes get hung up, make-up gets taken off. What happened to spontaneity? Is that what happened to her marriage? Which marriage? But good sense tells you, if you don't get to those candles now, you never will and the next thing you know, the fire department is breaking down your door and you're half-dressed out in the street on the eleven o'clock news.

Naked together, the moment comes back—and front. Long and arduous and lusty. Did we snuff out all the candles? There were a lot of candles. What about the ones in the bathroom? So she got up to check while he fell asleep. Eventually, she slept, too. But not right away. She liked looking at him while he slept. Maybe because for those brief moments he was her captive.

The morning shower together was strangely clinical after the previous night's activity. She had an empty feeling. Probably just hunger. Over coffee and English muffins, he looked at her and very seriously announced he needed a wife. She said nothing. Was it a proposal? He left for the TV studio, saying he had work to do.

She felt lonely because it was Sunday.

Dating is not marriage. Dating is not marriage. Dating is not marriage.

She got that. But she didn't really get it.

She came up with what she thought was a brilliant idea and got to work at her computer. At least she was writing. At last. At his place the following Friday evening, she handed him a formal resume for the job of his wife. She thought she was a perfect candidate and explained all that in her bio. He read the sheet of paper and smiled broadly. In British terms, he was roaring with laughter.

Nothing was mentioned about her job application to become Brenda Bolton. She didn't bring it up. He hadn't said anything. She thought it was a brilliant idea. She loved the alliteration of her name. B.B. She just took it that he needed time. That was it. She'd planted the seed. He would come 'round in time. He didn't mention it at all. Ever. Was she supposed to bring it up again? She didn't. Ever.

As the sex hotted up, as she surrendered to his ardent ways, he cooled in every other way. You can have my body, but not me. Where was fidelity, safety, trust, love, companionship? Not with this bloke. Why did he have to be so damned handsome, so damned English, so damned charming, so damned witty, so damned rich, so damned smart, so damned cold? She was more alone with him than when she was alone. She began to long for Ben. Even Tom would do. Was she totally nuts?

Harmony fell into discord. Ease became dis-ease. Hadn't she been here before? Was it her marriage resume joke that wasn't really a joke? Something happened. That is, nothing happened. One week, two weeks, three weeks, four weeks, five weeks, six weeks. Was Peter dead? She conned herself big time.

He's working hard. He's out of town. He feels too much for me. I've become a distraction and he can't do his work. He's afraid he'll get hurt. He has stuff going on. Boy, did he have stuff going on. Her heart wanted to call him. Her head said don't. Be patient. Her head was on vacation.

She made the call, hating herself the whole time.

He was warm and chatty as if nothing, absolutely nothing, was amiss.

"Let's have lunch," he said brightly.

"Okay," she chirped, convinced nothing was wrong. Did she really believe that? No.

"I'll tell you my good news." Cheery as could be he was.

"What news?" Naïve as could be she was.

"I'm getting married," he said. Just like that. No lead in; just like she was a mate at work.

"What!" she shouted into the phone.

"What?" he repeated.

"What happened to lunch?" she asked.

"Lunch?"

"You were going to tell me your news over lunch."

"Well, you know, the excitement of it all. Couldn't contain myself."

Barely giving the sonofabitch time to respond after each of her questions that started with who, what, when, how, why, her throat was trying to recover from an alleged stuck fish bone. But really, she had no strings on him. What was she really upset about? They weren't exactly engaged.

"Just one of those things, Brenda," he went on.

"Just one of those things."

"One of our new writers. Much younger. Twenty-something. It's a fairytale romance. Luck, actually."

"Lucky you." Bastard.

The lady in Brenda congratulated him.

The gentleman thanked her.

The woman scorned asked, "What would you like for a wedding present beside a hatchet?" Not wanting anything more to do with him, she clicked off and threw her phone on the sofa.

Without any time to recover, later that day, she opened her mail. Another blow. The divorce papers from what's-his-name. A piece of paper and it's over. It could be two years or fifty years, a piece of paper says it's over. A piece of paper says it is the beginning of wedded life and a piece of paper says it is the end of wedded life. Busy little paper. Bloody paper. Abandoned twice in one day. The tears came until there were none left.

She looked in the mirror. Not bad. Even when she cried, she was pretty. How fickle she was. The night before, she wanted to kill herself because she was convinced she looked like Woody Allen.

nger and loneliness followed. Actually, she was deal-ing with anger, too angry to be lonely. She'd been dou-ble-whammed smack in the face. Again. Her first thought was to call Ben. See if they could get back together. She needed a friend. But she didn't do it. She didn't call him. Hooray for her. She felt totally whacked out of her mind. Just a chemical imbalance. Whatever it was, it propelled her to get back on track with her writing. She fired up the com-puter. It can't be explained. It just came. From God? A gift? Maybe just a way of not being lonely. Could she only write when she was miserable? Does happiness stifle creativity? Another topic to tackle, but not today.

I'm alive and well and living in New York. I'm alive and well and living in New York. I'm alive and well and living in New York. And I'm sensational.

Writing is only about twenty percent of the job. Eighty percent is re-writing. She quickly made notes. First the ideas, then the characters, then the words, then the exact words, then sentences, then dialogue. At first, gibberish, then a shape. The what-ifs so on and so forth. Decisions, decisions, decisions.

An idea was forming. Something about being with someone for a while, even a long time, loving that person, finding out more about them. That thing you never knew. It was there all along when you didn't know, when you loved that person. But you find out. Does it change your feelings? The fantasy we caress of who the other person is so they fit into our pre-conceived idea of who we should be. Then the warts appear. You find out more. Then what? Stay? Go?

This was the premise. There was no Ben, no Tom, no Peter. Only her new characters, her new friends: Tina and Stavros. For some reason, it had to be Greek. Her recent entire diet of Greek yogurt maybe? She was very impressionable. More than likely, it was the piece she read in the newspaper and saw in the news about Cyprus. It was big. Something about it interested her. She couldn't explain it. She liked her Greek grocer. But she didn't want to write about a grocer. She knew she wanted a main character with an accent. She'd never been to Cyprus, but contrary to some believers you only can write what you know first-hand, she got what she needed by reading up on the subject. Weeks and weeks of research. She didn't have a team of researchers. She did it all herself. And her Greek grocer was helpful, too.

Working titles: Greeks Bearing Gifts. The Nightgown.

Brief Synopsis: The play takes place just after the invasion of Cyprus in July, 1974 by the Turks. The Greeks were displaced and we learn that it was the Americans and the British who aided the event. But this isn't a political play. It's about a man and a woman who are lovers. He, it turns out, is involved in this invasion. She's recovering from surgery. A hysterectomy. No. An appendectomy. He reveals who he is. The nightgown turns him on and loosens his tongue.

STAVROS SKARLATIDES, 50, visits his girlfriend, TINA PRIMOS, about ten years younger than he is, in the hospital in New York. She is recovering from an appendectomy. He has come to propose marriage after their twelve month courtship. This, she would have accepted. But, and it's a big but, he reveals to her who he really is, something his late wife was not aware of and Tina is suddenly very frightened, suddenly not knowing the man she has known, the man she has loved.

"Did you think I was a shoe salesman?" he snaps. "I make the shoes, darling."

"You're Greek. I assumed shipping and commodities," she answers meekly.

Do our feelings change because we find out more about someone we've known and loved? She says they do. He says they don't.

Brenda re-wrote her preliminary notes at least a dozen times. It was coming fast. The first act would just involve two characters. Maybe it was just a one-act. She was confident all would be revealed as she kept working on it. Her characters would tell her what they wanted. And then it came to her. What did she have holding her at home? She needed to travel to the place she was writing about. It wasn't enough to read what others had written about Cyprus. She needed to soak it all up in person. She had to be there. She wanted to be there. She couldn't explain the pull it had on her. What was waiting for her there? She had to find out. A week, ten days, a month. Whatever it took. She wanted to smell it, see it, feel it, hear it, taste it. All she had to do was make the reservations. Out of courtesy, she left a message for Ben, relieved it was just his voice mail. No doubt he would return the call, but she didn't have to pick up. Caller-ID was awesome.

Money isn't any good just sitting around doing nothing. She had to go. If not now, when? She needed to find a real Stavros.

PART III

29

Cyprus was the third largest island in the Mediterranean. The island was divided by an invasion in 1974. This was the thread of her play. She was obsessed by it. And isn't that what Hemingway said? You have to write what's burning up inside you. Nothing she read in a book or in a newspaper or saw online or on television could match up to actually being there.

Flying into Larnaca Airport was thrilling. She was a writer going to the place she was going to write about. There was no need to make decisions by committee. It was all her and it was wonderful. The weather was glorious in late September—sunny and hot, slowly moving into autumn's warm days and cool evenings, but still warm enough to swim. It was her second major trip solo, Paris being the first, and looked what happened with that!

She liked how she felt even if she was slightly apprehensive about her choice of accommodations, having opted for a small, family run hotel in the mountains, easily accessed by an airport shuttle, about a thirty-five minute ride. It seemed to have everything a writer would need in the way of privacy. And it was close to the main street of the village; within walking distance of the larger fancier hotel, where non-guests could swim without paying the high price of a room. Safe.

According to the brochure, there were eighty rooms, all with balconies, on five floors. Ceiling fans took the place of central air. If there was any air conditioning, it was not evident. She had missed the summer months when families, a mix of nationalities, took their holiday, so the hotel wasn't full. And there was a restaurant. All quite acceptable.

She was pleased at how easy it was to make new friends. The inhabitants were curious about the American traveling alone. The fact that she was a playwright, definitely not a journalist or reporter, intrigued them. There was Ziad from Egypt, another guest at the hotel. They would drink ginger ales together on the patio and chat. His English was excellent. It turned out he had a brother in North Carolina. Did Brenda know him? A pediatrician at Brenner Children's Hospital. She didn't know him, but did know about Wake Forest Baptist Medical Center in Winston-Salem. He kept insisting she had it all wrong. Brenda had to work hard at explaining the Brenner wing was part of the hospital and that New York and North Carolina were not that close.

Ziad invited her to the Curium Theatre, just outside Limassol, to see a British production of Shakespeare's *A Midsummer Night's Dream* done every year running, for two nights, to raise money for the Committee on Chest Diseases. The well-intentioned amateurs played to an enthusiastic crowd. It meant an overnight stay as Limassol was a bit of a way from Platres, but Ziad assured her she would have her own room at a small hotel near the theatre. And he kept his word. Then she found out his leanings were towards the male gender, which had to be kept secret for all sorts of reasons, and that was just fine with her.

This little hotel in Platres was just the ticket, so she thought, until the evening she returned from the dining room having spent an hour chatting to a couple from Italy who were on their honeymoon. It was hot, hotter than usual for this time of year in the mountains, and there wasn't any air conditioning. To get any air at all, it was necessary to keep the balcony door in her room open; not a good idea, since it attracted unwanted guests. She was not enamored of insects flying into her room. But it was better than the oppressive heat.

This particular evening, she returned to her room after dinner and a giant lizard-like animal was on the ceiling. She spotted it as soon as she opened her door. It was huge. Okay, a small gecko. She didn't like it. It was late and no one was around so she raced to the kitchen to get help. A young waiter, or perhaps the pastry chef for all she knew, followed her to her room, climbed up on a chair, and with his bare hands lifted the thing up and tossed it over the balcony. His English wasn't very good, but he said something about the lizard being a good thing because it ate insects; at least that's what she thought he said.

They stood very close to one another. His eyes were as light blue as the sea. He said some words in Greek that she didn't understand, but he was so handsome, it didn't matter. As the saying goes, it was all Greek to her. They had their own way of communicating. She never did get his name. He called her something that sounded like Mrs. Garden. No doubt all the guests were known to the hotel staff. She couldn't believe what was happening, and she was the one in the picture. And she still couldn't believe it. He really was the handsomest man she had ever seen.

After, they smoked. After the after, she kept everything closed. She thought it might be a good idea to make arrangements to move to another hotel.

Around eleven the next morning, Brenda walked over to the tourist office in the village. She loved this place. She imagined herself living in New York six months of the year and in Platres six months of the year. She could rent a small villa. She wouldn't need much. A few personal items, a few sets of clothes, a laptop computer. Was the idea so outrageous? Sure, it took money, but this wasn't an issue. There was money. She'd have to talk to Ben, of course, but what reason would he have to object? He never said he would support her only if she lived in New York. It was a great idea. She would study the Greek language, immerse herself in the culture, become part of the village community, and best of all, she would write. On the back cover of her books, it would list homes in New York and Cyprus. Her plays would be full of interesting characters pulled from both cultures.

Brenda was offered a coffee at the tourist office. She welcomed it as she had skipped breakfast at the hotel. Without going into detail, she said simply that she wanted to change hotels. Brenda and Irene, the agent, clicked immediately. About sixty, Irene explained that she worked part-time in the tourist office. Rather pretty, in a coarse way, with a dark complexion, short, black hair with just a touch of gray at the temples, a shrill voice when she got excited, she told Brenda that she took the job because she loved organizing people. Brenda told Irene that she was a writer and was here to do research for a new play.

In Brenda's experience, when anyone met a writer, they would relate details about their life unintentionally or intentionally thinking it would make a good story. Irene didn't let her down. She started to talk about the invasion.

"I was in Nicosia in the north, saw the parachutes coming down. We never heard the planes because they were so high. Just suddenly the parachutes were falling everywhere. The bombs were coming all around our house." Her eyes misted over. "All the Greek Cypriots were displaced from homes, from businesses. That's why we are here in the southern part of the island. All these years. We kept thinking we would go back to our homes any time. It still hasn't happened. Everything was abandoned. Businesses, shops. My parents had a little grocery store. Everybody had to leave. Had to leave our furniture and everything. I was only a teenager. You know what they did? They drew a line down the middle to separate the north from the south part of the island. I heard it was called the Green Line. I don't know why. A lifetime has gone by. I can never forget. It is still difficult to talk about it. But we made a life here. We had to. I married another refugee, we have a daughter, and we live in hope. Still. That's my life."

This information was better than gold. It was Brenda's reason for coming here.

"But now to business," Irene said. "You want to change hotels."

"I need air conditioning. Allergies, you understand. That's the only reason. Otherwise I'd stay where I am," Brenda lied.

Irene didn't have to think very long. "Forest Park. Family owned since 1936. Like an American hotel. You'll love it."

"I know it. That's where I swim every day," Brenda said, excited about the prospect of moving up while apprehensive about the cost. "Pricey?"

"It is four-star, big, and pricey, yes, with all modern conveniences, but not to worry. I am friends with the owner, and the season is quieting down. I'm sure we can get a special deal."

The move from one hotel to another was seamless, thanks to Irene. The suite offered Brenda was actually an upgrade from a small room at the same price. And not much more than what she was paying now. Without the geckos. Nothing changes in the world. It's who you know. Brenda made a mental note to buy Irene a gift to say thank-you.

Two days later, Brenda went to the tourist office and presented a beautiful pale turquoise silk scarf to Irene who just loved it saying it wasn't necessary. Putting the scarf around her neck, she said she would cherish it.

"Well, tell me, how do you like your new accommodations?" Irene asked.

"I'm thrilled. It wouldn't have happened without you."

"It was a pleasure to help. This time of year, the room would have stayed empty, believe me. So it all worked out."

"Yes."

"And you are right there near the pool any time you feel like a swim."

"I love it. It's all wonderful. Am I dreaming?"

"It's real, my dear. And now, I have an invitation for you. I was going to ring you, but it is better in person."

"Oh?" Brenda was up for anything.

"In three days, we have the Baptism of a baby boy. The mother, Aphrodite, is a friend of my daughter, so I must go. And you must come as my guest. It will be a wonderful experience. You can write about it. Plenty of good food. And an opportunity where we all get dressed up."

"I'd love it! You know, Irene, things are working here for me. I can't explain it. I have this incredible feeling something extraordinary is going to happen. It is very important to be here now. I don't know why but I believe that. Am I crazy?"

"Believe your feelings. You never know what is around the corner."

"And they say New York is the center of the world. My social life isn't this good in Manhattan."

You can be the one who rings the bell, Brenda," Irene said with pride. They were standing outside the monastery in a village near Platres.

"Me? Are you sure?"

"Of course."

Brenda looked for the bell. "I don't see a bell."

"Not like on a house. Look up. Up."

Brenda looked up. "Oh."

"Just pull the chain. Go ahead."

Brenda wished she had a photo of that in her little black dress and high heels. It was a first. She wasn't sure how long to keep ringing, so she just kept pulling the chain until Irene told her to stop. They went inside and joined the others.

Brenda felt part of it all, not like an outsider. She was even given a candle to hold like everyone else. The heat was melting the wax very fast. All the candles were twisted. It was rather a funny sight that didn't go unnoticed by the attendees.

Thanks to Irene's running translation, Brenda didn't miss a moment of the forty-five minute ceremony. The baby's father was allowed inside, but—according to custom—the mother had to stay outside the church. The godfather looked very pleased. An Armenian, it had been necessary for him to obtain special permission to be the godfather and appear in a Greek Orthodox ceremony. When the Priest was about to dip the baby in the olive oil and water, the grandmother shouted out, in Greek, of course, that the water was too hot.

The Priest nearly physically pushed the woman away saying, "Are you doing this Christening or am I?"

Brenda was sure Irene had cleaned up the translation a little because it got a great big laugh from the guests. Father Niklos was a slight man with rather a devilish look, jolly light eyes, white hair tied back in a ponytail. His white beard, yellow really, didn't match his hair. Brenda surmised he might be a smoker. His age was hard to determine. Fifty or sixty. The ponytail was a nice touch.

After the church ceremony, everyone went into the pine grove for the meze and beer. Lots of beer as it turned out. About seventy people sat on the ground and put paper plates with food on the cloths laid out. Brenda preferred to sit on the cloth and hold the plate in her lap. There was some singing and suddenly, after much drink, much food, and a lot of cigarettes, Father Niklos belted out a number, a piece of bread hanging from his lips.

Brenda didn't speak all day, just listened to the Greek language which she didn't understand, ate a lot of food she didn't like, and smiled at a lot of people she didn't know. Still, it was an experience not to have been missed. She returned to her hotel tired and needing a hot bath despite the heat and humidity. She decided to go for a swim in the pool instead. A few laps would work off some of the calories, calm her, and mentally get her ready for sleep.

It had been a special day. As her head hit the pillow, her last thoughts were on the little, handmade white suit she'd seen in a shop window in the village. It would be a perfect gift for the newly Christened baby boy named Antony. Just before drifting off, in her opinion, the mother with most unfortunate looks should not have been named Aphrodite, the Greek goddess of love and beauty.

Brenda woke up refreshed with that wonderful feeling that something extraordinary was going to happen. It was something about this place she was sure. After a delicious breakfast of two poached eggs on toast and black coffee, she headed for the pool. She brought her notebook so she could write.

Climbing out of the shallow end of the pool, she noticed him for the first time lounging in the chair next to hers. Had he been watching her? She couldn't be sure. Where had he come from? The hotel? It must have been while she was swimming. Was he another guest? He looked like he belonged there. The owner or a family member? No, that wasn't it. She'd had similar feelings before about men, not always acting on them, but this was different. Exactly how different she couldn't explain. Trying to look like she wasn't staring at him, she ascertained he had a medium build, was middle-aged, whatever that was these days, had light brown hair, and was nice looking without being handsome. As he was sitting, it was hard to tell how tall he was. Anyway, what did any of this matter? Yet, she was drawn to him. And as their eyes met, it was obvious, so was he drawn to her. She knew even if she hadn't said the first 'hello' he would have.

And there it was. The happening. Her Cyprus affair. He

was called Markos, but Brenda knew she may have met her fictional character, Stavros. Markos was a diplomat. That's all he would reveal. He didn't talk very much about his personal life except to say he had a wife. They lived in a villa near the hotel and he always swam at Forest Park when he was in residence. His job kept him away most of the time. There was a moment when Brenda could have prevented or stopped the connection. He was a married man and in her book that was a non-event. But she let the moment slip by. She couldn't stop it any more than she could stop breathing.

Their liaisons took place in her suite at the hotel. Brenda didn't ask how he could come and go like that with his villa a stone's throw away, with his wife waiting for him at home, with everyone knowing who he was. The point is the man gave of himself and for that, Brenda was grateful. He opened up to her and showed her she still had the ability to make another human being happy.

He was intelligent, sensitive—a child in many ways. They talked of meeting in Limassol at a place they could be alone to swim, play tennis, and make love. They talked about meeting in New York during one of his trips. They talked about a lot of things. She told him she would send him her writings. He said he would love it.

"We are together in bed, my American woman. You take something from me, I take something from you. You is you and me is me. The one thing you cannot be is me. The one thing I cannot be is you. But we are each now something more because you gave to me and I gave to you."

It was all cozy until Brenda met his wife early one evening at the village café where husband and wife were sitting and conversing with friends. It was the custom on a Sunday evening to stroll and sit at the café with other locals. And she adored the woman almost instantly, hating what she was doing with her husband.

Maud was beautiful. Surprisingly, she was many years older than Markos. Brenda got the feeling there was a mental illness, not necessarily hers but someone close. Brenda sensed she was artistic in some way. All of these speculations were confirmed later by Markos. Maud had devoted her life, after her parents died, to a mentally ill sister. And Maud had been a concert pianist. Maud took to Brenda and invited her to the villa to have tea with her and Markos the next day.

What is this web I'm being sucked into? Brenda wrote in her journal. *He's married. I've met the wife. Does she know about me? I don't even know about me. Who am I now?*

She justified her actions by telling herself it was a writer's job to explore, experience, say yes to everything. And oh, was she crazy about Stavros. Of course, she meant Markos.

They were sitting in the garden of the villa. Markos and Maud's villa. Markos and Maud. It would never be Markos and Brenda. What was she playing at? Brenda was afraid she'd give it all away by looking at Markos. If their eyes met, their passion would surface. So she focused on Maud, hoping she wasn't overdoing it. Her mind was working overtime.

After twenty-five years of marriage, how can you not sense something is going on between your husband and me? You are strong, ultra-sensitive, and quite beautiful with your long pearls on a simple gray dress and white hair pulled back in a chignon. I hope I look like you at your age. Oh, dear, I like you so much. You are both one for me. This is all so crazy.

Maud liked Brenda. Otherwise, why would she show her the poetry she wrote? Why would she play the piano for her? Markos stood by listening as his wife talked about her music, her sewing, and her knitting. "Shall we have tea now? Markos?"

Markos disappeared into the kitchen.

"He is always in charge of the tea. And in the morning, he makes the most wonderful coffee. Then he likes to go the hotel for a swim. In two weeks, we will leave for Belgium. I don't always go with him on his trips, but there is nothing to keep me here, and he does need me to attend the functions with him."

Brenda didn't ask what kind of functions. She wanted to leave, but she was intrigued by Maud. She was learning about Markos through Maud. About them.

"I think you will understand this. When I have my music and my poetry, I don't need anything else," Maud said. "Ah, here is Markos with the tea."

"It's the same for me with my writing. I spend days alone not really aware of being alone," Brenda said accepting the tea from Markos without looking at him.

"But you are still young. You need someone on the same wavelength. A companion, a friend." Maud and Markos looked at one another and smiled. She thanked him for the tea.

"I can't imagine anyone again on a permanent basis."

"Perhaps you haven't found the right one until now."

What did 'until now' mean? Was that when Maud nodded her head towards Markos? Or was it Brenda's guilty conscience?

Am I a younger version of her? No. I operate in a more physical way. I think I am stronger than she is. She is sensational. Is he? We three are one. I am her and I am him. It's too wild. The whole thing is dangerous and complicated. Don't let it be either, Brenda. You can back out now.

Then he took the floor and made them laugh with his stories. The Indian Chief. The false teeth. The actor-diplomat. The false teeth story brought tears to Brenda and Maud. Brenda wouldn't remember any of the details but she loved being entertained this way. For her money, Markos could talk and talk and talk and talk. And she was thanking God that he was talking. It meant she didn't have to.

Why can't I have it all except for the physical attraction?

Then there would be no danger. Maybe they aren't married. She's not his wife. They say that to keep the women away. And together they meet the woman who is right for him and reveal all. No. No. No. No. Very wrong, wrong, wrong. She is his wife. She isn't worried about me as a threat to her marriage. I'm a mere insignificant passing moment; she is forever.

All these thoughts were giving Brenda a headache.

Maybe I just need my mother. Maybe I miss Ben. My head is killing me. Thank God I leave day after tomorrow.

When the three finally said their goodbyes, Brenda promised Maud she would write, knowing she never would.

Markos walked Brenda to the door.

"Maud will die before me. I will remarry a younger woman and she will have affairs and I will be so jealous. And that's the way it is." He kissed Brenda on both cheeks, took her face in his hands and whispered, "Thank you."

Brenda did not know what he meant. "Thank you, too."

She wasn't successful in masking her tears. She needn't have bothered. For Markos, the interlude had passed. Brenda was not going to be wife number two. He was back in his life before Brenda was on the other side of the door. Still, she didn't regret anything that had happened between them. Her recovery powers were good. She'd had a lot of practice.

PART IV

The Nightgown
By Brenda Gordon

CHARACTERS

TINA: 40's. Single. Greek American. Lives in Manhattan. Recovering from an appendectomy. Groggy from medication, but not incoherent. Wears a drab hospital nightgown.

STAVROS: 50's. Widowed. Tina's affluent cultured Greek lover. A slight accent. Lives mostly in Athens when he's in one place. Wears a conservative suit, shirt, and tie.

SCENE

Private room in a New York City hospital. A narrow bed, a chair, a bedside table.

TIME

Early afternoon Saturday the 20th of July, 1974.

AT RISE: TINA is in hospital in a private room. She is lying in bed in a semi-dozed state. STAVROS enters quietly. Takes her in adoringly with his eyes. Well-groomed, a little weary, he carries a small oblong gift-wrapped box.

                    TINA

                    (Opens her eyes slowly.
                    Happily surprised to see
                    him)

Stavros! You're here!

                    STAVROS

Melly-moo. (Greek term of endearment)

                    (Gets on bed; attempts to
                    fondle her)

                    TINA

                    (Gently pushes him away)

No. Too soon. (Reaches for the gift) For me?

                    STAVROS

                    (Takes gift from her and
                    puts it on bedside table)

Later, darling. Enjoy the anticipation. It is
part of the gift.

                    TINA

Stavros.

                    STAVROS

Darling! Three weeks is too long. I've missed
you.

                    TINA

                    (Lets him embrace her, but
                    is in no condition for this
                    physicality, settles for a
                    kiss, and then gently pushes
                    him away again)

It hurts. Don't press.

                    STAVROS

Sorry.

> (Moves off the bed, looks
> around for the chair, moves
> it closer to the bed, sits.
> He is up and down during
> their dialogue)

TINA

You look tired. Rough flight?

STAVROS

> (Waves his hand in the air)

It's nothing. My body is accustomed to
unconventional hours. In Athens, as children
we would sleep all day so we could go out
at night. We were in the streets playing at
midnight. No one sleeps in Athens. You don't
know how much I love that place. It's in my
blood. When you come there, you will see.

TINA

My mother used to tell me stories of how she
and her mother would wait at home for the men.

> (Brief silence)

I didn't know you were coming. I would have
dressed. (Jokingly refers to her hospital
gown)

STAVROS

You look beautiful.

TINA

It's true. Love is blind.

STAVROS

Love is all there is.

> (Wants to kiss her, but
> keeps his distance)

How is everything down there?

                    TINA

I'm now minus one appendix and I'm alive. I
was lucky we caught it before it burst. And
that it wasn't more serious.

                    STAVROS

You are in pain?

                    TINA

Nothing like what it was. They say I can go
home tomorrow.

                    STAVROS

And make love. How I've missed you.

                    TINA

                    (Sorrier for him than for
                    her)

Six to eight weeks the doctor said.

                    STAVROS

The trials and tribulations of love.

                    TINA

We can make out on the couch like teenagers.

                    STAVROS

                    (Doesn't share her sense of
                    humor)

No matter. I leave tomorrow for London.

                    TINA

You came in for only one day to see me?

                    STAVROS

Business, darling. Always business. And of
course you.

                    TINA

You seem preoccupied.

                    STAVROS

Actually, it is true. I am preoccupied.
(Not sure how much to say) I've been in
negotiations for twenty hours straight.

                    TINA

Negotiations?

                    STAVROS

At the Waldorf.

                    TINA

The Waldorf? How long have you been in New
York?

                    STAVROS

A secret meeting.

                    TINA

At the Waldorf? It isn't exactly a hideaway
motel.

                    STAVROS

Exactly. We all look like we belong there.
Just regular travelers. We rouse no suspicion.
The king has a suite. It appears to be simply
a visit to pay one's respects.

                    TINA

King is his first name, right?

                    STAVROS

Don't play the fool. A king of a country
the name of which I am positively unable to
reveal to you. A British General, a priest, a
scientist, a newspaper magnate, and a Greek.
Six of us. We have meetings.

                    TINA

I know I'm medicated, but I think I heard you.
Meetings about what?

STAVROS

Nothing. World events. End of story. I'd much
rather talk about you.

TINA

That's it? You can't leave me hanging like
that, telling me only part of the story.

STAVROS

(Studies her before speaking)
Five days ago, Turkey invaded Cyprus.

TINA

And this has what to do with you?

STAVROS

That is what I do.

TINA

We've been seeing each other nearly twelve
months. You never mentioned, well, what you
said about meetings, a king, Cyprus. For the
first time, I don't know what you do.

STAVROS

I'm a businessman. You know that.

TINA

You never even hinted at meetings about world
events. You are now a man of mystery.

STAVROS

Rubbish. From the moment we met at the Greek
American Ball you know Stavros Skarlatides,
the man. Stavros Skarlatides, the businessman
is different. Few know him. My wife knew
nothing of my business. We were so young…
(A moment of remorse) Even now my son does
not know all the facts. My mother is another
story. She knows all.

                    TINA

Your mother? Present tense?

                    STAVROS

What are you talking about?

                    TINA

You never mentioned her. I assumed she was -
dead.

                    STAVROS

She lives in my house at the beach south of
Athens. After my wife died, I never went
there, so I moved my mother, my brother, and
his wife into the house.

                    TINA

She's well?

                    STAVROS

Why do Americans have this idea once you reach
seventy-five you should be sick? My mother is
eighty-three, does all the cooking, shopping,
cleaning. The sea air will keep her alive to
one hundred and twenty.

                         (Momentarily closes his
                         eyes. He is weary)

                    TINA

Stavros?

                    STAVROS

                         (Opens his eyes)

Nay? (Greek for yes)

                    TINA

Stavros, what's going on?

STAVROS

> (It is a few beats before he answers)

We had to decide what to do about Cyprus. The plan went wrong. All we wanted was a tax haven.

TINA

We? You're frightening me.

STAVROS

The invasion. It was on the news, in the papers.

TINA

I must have missed it. I was under the knife, remember?

STAVROS

Turkey invaded Cyprus and got only half the island. The north. We were supposed to conquer the entire island and throw all the Greeks out. Something happened. The Americans… never mind. Over two hundred thousand Cypriots were-are-displaced.

TINA

Why would Americans be involved? Stavros, are you a spy? Is it dangerous for you to be here?

STAVROS

No to both questions.

TINA

You didn't answer my first question.

STAVROS

There was an invasion. Who do you think supplied the money, the planes?

                    TINA

The Americans?

                  STAVROS

And the British.

                    TINA

But this is preposterous. Cyprus is a tiny
insignificant island over there somewhere.

                  STAVROS

Do you know where Turkey is?

                    TINA

                    (Has to think about it)

Next to Russia.

                  STAVROS

America has missiles in Turkey.

                    TINA

So? Oh. Russia. Ah.

                  STAVROS

Ah, indeed. The Americans must be able to
keep their missiles in Turkey; therefore,
relations with Turkey must be kept friendly.
Cyprus still remains under British influence
and Britain needs to stay on good terms with
America. You see how it works?

                    TINA

Britain needs America and the Brits help out,
so to speak.

                  STAVROS

Cyprus is right in the middle. Turkey invades
Cyprus. The Greeks go back to Greece. American
missiles stay in Turkey. And let's not forget
Russia. That was the plan. Something happened.

All the criminals in Turkey were supposed
to be sent to Cyprus. Cyprus would just be
an island for all the Turkish rubbish. And
everyone would be happy.

TINA

What about the Cypriots? They wouldn't be
happy.

STAVROS

We didn't expect what happened. There was
a coup just before the invasion. President
Makarios was replaced and his men went with
him to jail which left no fighting men on the
island. Many of the pilots were British. There
were no fighter planes. What no one expected,
with Makarios and his men out of the way, was
that the Turks were held back by the women and
children; the old men; the priests. They were
determined to keep the land, risking their
lives against bombs.

TINA

Those poor people. Their homes, their lives.
But what has this got to do with you?

STAVROS

Have you not heard me?

TINA

Oh… my… God!

> (She is speechless. Wants
> to get up, but her attempt
> fails due to pain. He isn't
> sure how to help. She waves
> his hand away)

STAVROS

We work for the total good of mankind. That is
the objective.

TINA

That explains all the travel. London, New
York, Rome, Switzerland. Will the real Stavros
Skarlatides stand up?

STAVROS

(Doesn't get reference to TV
show)

What are you talking about? You know me. I am
the same man you've known for twelve months.
We make love. You know me, melly-moo.

TINA

It's just a game to you.

STAVROS

He who has not discovered that all of life is
a game is to be pitied. And it is a pity you
favor your American side. What has happened to
your Greek roots? Americans take themselves
too seriously.

TINA

You're damned right we do.

STAVROS

No, no, my darling. It is responsibilities
that must be taken seriously, not ourselves.

TINA

What happens now?

STAVROS

There is a dividing line from one end of the
island to the other, dividing the Greek and
the Turkish zones.

TINA

They are separated now?

STAVROS

The Turks moved into the northern part of the island; the Greeks are refugees now, in the southern part. Anyone who attempts to cross the line is killed.

TINA

How? By whom?

STAVROS

There are guards. They have been instructed to shoot anyone who attempts to cross the line. The only way to get into Cyprus is through Istanbul. No one can enter from the Greek side.

TINA

This is devastating. I haven't been that interested in history but this is about you. Us.

STAVROS

It does not affect us.

TINA

Doesn't affect us? I know because you have told me. What I want to know is who am I in all this?

STAVROS

You are my wonderful Tina with only one fault. You are American. In here (pointing to her head).

TINA

And proud of it.

STAVROS

I feel that way about being Greek. Our Russian scientist feels that way about being Russian. So on and so forth.

                    TINA

Everyone wants to be American.

                  STAVROS

No, darling. That is American marketing. By
the way, Makarios escaped.

                    TINA

By the way? How can you be so nonchalant?

                  STAVROS

          (Basking in the glory of who
          he is)

Today is the 20th of July. In three days, the
President of Greece will dismiss his Cabinet
and recall the self-exiled Konstantinos
Karamanlis to form a new government. On
the same day, Sampson will be relieved of
his post and the president of the House of
Representatives, Glafkos Clerides, will be
made the interim president. I fly to London
tomorrow, to Geneva on Monday. A meeting
with the three guarantors of the Cyprus
Constitution: Great Britain, Greece, and
Turkey, about the exchange of prisoners and
the relocation of refugees. There will be
several cease fire agreements, but none will
be -

                    TINA

          (Interrupts him)

Stop!

                  STAVROS

          (Ignores her pleas)

None will be effective. Makarios will return
later this year to resume the presidency. In
February, 1975, the Turkish Cypriots will

proclaim their occupied area to be a separate
state under *Rauf Denktash*.

                    TINA

Why are you here? To tell me this?

                   STAVROS

No. Today, melly-moo, I came here only to ask
you a very important question. I want you to
be my wife.

                    TINA

Marry you?

                   STAVROS

That is a question. What is your answer?

                    TINA

And if I say no, do you have me killed?

                   STAVROS

No time for jokes.

                    TINA

I'm not laughing. Last week, I wouldn't have
hesitated to accept your marriage proposal. I
always hoped we would get married. But now,
that's all changed.

                   STAVROS

Nothing is changed. We loved each other last
month, and we love each other today. I own
homes in Greece. You can keep your New York
apartment. You never have to work if you don't
want to.

                    TINA

You think you can run me the way you run the
world? It's outrageous what you've told me and
even more outrageous that you expect me to
marry you.

STAVROS

You think what I've told you is outrageous?
Watch the news and learn.

TINA

I'm beyond that now. I'm talking about two
human beings who happen to be us. Please go. I
don't sleep with strangers.

STAVROS

What is the matter with you? You know who I
am.

TINA

You're Greek. I thought shipping; commodities.

STAVROS

The American in you has the shoe salesman
mentality. I don't sell the shoes, darling. I
make the shoes.

TINA

This is insane. How can I marry you? I loved
you once; that's the man I thought I would
marry. Hoped to marry.

STAVROS

You don't suddenly stop loving someone because
you know more about them. I have not changed
since the day you met me. I was a member
of the Six then. Now you know it. Then you
didn't. I'm the same person I was before I
came into this room and told you.

TINA

It's not the knowing. It's what I know that
frightens me.

STAVROS

To be Greek is not to be afraid.

TINA

You can't twist this around. What would happen
if you and the others are found out? And now I
know. What happens to me?

STAVROS

You are safe. We are cautious. Besides, who
would believe it? By the way, did I tell
you we are calling the dividing line The
Green Line? Leave it to the Americans. At the
meeting, I was drawing on a map and only a
green marking pen was available. The American
newspaperman came up with the name. The Green
Line. It will look good in print, he said. Be
my wife, Tina Primos.

TINA

Go away, whoever you are. It's all changed
now. Everything's changed.

STAVROS

It would not matter to me if you told me you
had eight husbands and poisoned them all. I
would still be madly in love with you.

TINA

I think it would bother you a little.

STAVROS

The heart does not change. Hearts meet. Hearts
love.

TINA

Some kind of Greek myth?

STAVROS

What I have told you is real.

TINA

I've heard enough. You frighten me. Your world
is very far away.

STAVROS

You think because American soil has never
known war, it can't happen. Wait and see.

TINA

I'm in no condition for this. I've had my
insides taken out. You only care how soon you
can get laid. You don't care about me.

STAVROS

It doesn't suit you to be crude. Of course I
care. I'm here.

TINA

And that's your answer. You are here. And you
want me to marry you on that.

STAVROS

I love you, Tina. You make my life complete.

TINA

You've shattered my life. Why now? Why today?
Why have you revealed all this to me now?
After a year together. Why now?

STAVROS

That damned nightgown.

TINA

My nightgown?

STAVROS

Beautiful. No make-up, so natural, so
innocent. I feel aroused. It made me want to
unburden myself.

TINA

An ugly hospital gown turns you on?

STAVROS

I find it so damned sexy. It loosened my tongue.

Not about the proposal, as you will see when you unwrap the gift. That was my plan. I only came to ask you to marry me.

                    TINA

We never talked about marriage. I just always thought… hoped. But now that I've heard it out loud, I don't know.
I feel like I'm in the twilight zone. Please… please go.

                  STAVROS

Yes, you need to rest. I have some things to do while I'm in the city. I'll come back this evening. Never speak of this conversation except when we are face to face. Rest now. You will feel differently later. Love is all there is. Don't forget the gift.

                    (EXITS)

                  TINA

                  (After a beat, picks up the box)

I hope it isn't a bomb.

                  (Unwraps it. It is a beautiful diamond bracelet)

Holy Mother of God! One thing you can say about him. He isn't cheap.

                  LIGHTS OUT

35

Damn! Just as she was typing in a note about the title, possibly changing it to *Greeks Bearing Gifts*, the phone rang. She'd forgotten to turn it off. She didn't recognize the number. Usually wary of unrecognizable callers, she answered. It was the last person in the world she expected to hear from. Damn! What was he saying? Her mind was wrapped up in Tina and Stavros, but she caught the gist of it.

"The Mayfair affair didn't work out. I made a big mistake."

"Where are you calling from?" She didn't know why she even asked that question. She didn't care where he was. Her mind was on the play.

"I'm back in New York. There's talk about a Broadway production. My agent says there's interest. Bren, listen, we were too hasty. I want to get back together. Maybe not marriage, but we belong together. It was good once. It can be good again. Who knows? Re-marriage maybe. Liz and Dick did it twice. We really had something. I know it. We made a mistake, Brenda. We are meant to be together."

We? *We?* Her head was spinning. The smell of her cooked roast beef wafting through a tiny flat in London filled her nostrils, not to mention the slight smell of damp that was always with them, but which they had chosen to not exactly ignore, but to live with.

There is no we. There is no we. There is no we. What the hell was wrong with men?

"I'm working, Tom," she said with a clip. She was going to stick it to him. "You know how I am when I'm in the zone," she spat out, paraphrasing his words that had been like a knife to her heart that fateful evening in London. She clicked off making sure to turn off the ringer. He was an idiot. And she was done with idiots in her life.

Even if the flow had been interrupted, she had something. She knew it. She had a real first scene of a play. She was back, she was back. She was better than just back. She had moved forward to heights where she had never been. Unaware of time, unaware of space, she poured a glass of wine. She felt elated. Just for a split second, she had the feeling she wanted to share it with someone. But there was no one. At least, not anyone at the present time. But she wasn't alone. She had her characters. She had given life to people who wouldn't have existed without her. She didn't need real people. Funny, how creativity separates you from the world.

Suddenly, Ben loomed large. She had the greatest desire to call him, blaming it on the wine. They hadn't been all that great together, not for a long time, but they were far worse apart. No. Not true. She was absolutely fine. She was living her life. Okay, so Ben was supplying the monetary funds. Completely his choice. New York was an expensive town. She wasn't going to look a gift horse in the mouth.

And then a thought came to her. That guy Josh, the jogger, wasn't so wrong. She could actually get a job and still write. Oh, not selling cosmetics in a department store. At the University or the Writers Guild. Part-time. Why not? A lot of writers had other jobs. Then she wouldn't be so dependent on Ben. This was good. This was really good. Maybe a smaller apartment. She liked the apartment. She'd have to think that one through. She was growing. Definitely growing. You're never too old to grow up. A writer writes. And she knew her only failure in life would be not to use the gift she was given.

The doorbell.

Shit. Tom? It couldn't be. He wouldn't. She opened the door.

But it wasn't Tom.

He looked fantastic. Almost movie-esque. Richard Gere movie-esque. Why hadn't she seen that before? "Ben? I mean, Ben! It's you." She was completely bowled over.

"I hope you don't mind me dropping in without calling first. I was in the building."

"I'm working, but what the hell, I can take a break. Join me in a glass of red?"

"A little early for me, but thanks for asking."

"Well, we can stand in the entrance hall or you can come in and we can sit down in the living room like real people. I'll make a pot of tea." Why did she say that? He didn't drink tea. As far as she knew he didn't. Maybe he had started drinking tea. Why was she thinking about tea? Why didn't she say coffee? He liked coffee. She took another sip of her wine. She wasn't sure how to act. Glad? Mad? Cordial? Distant? Familiar? The truth was she was in awe. Had he always looked like this and she never saw it? But it wasn't just his physical presence. It was something else. An aura. She motioned for him to come in.

He followed her into the living room but they didn't sit down. She didn't make any tea. She didn't make coffee. They stood and looked at one another.

"Well, Ben. You're here. Because? Business or pleasure?"

How long had it been since they'd seen one another? She was relieved she wasn't in her ratty old bathrobe.

"A little of both you might say. I just negotiated a deal you won't believe. No one would believe it. I won't go into the how and why but I just got a ten-year lease for a client in this building for one hundred a month."

"One hundred dollars? In Manhattan? In this area?"

"That's what I said."

"Is it legal?"

"Absolutely above board. I'll spare you the details. What do you think of that?"

"I think it's impossible, but quite possibly marvelous."

"Well, I did it."

"Like six hundred square feet?"

"Much bigger. Quite decent. One bedroom, one bathroom, huge living and dining area, eat-in kitchen."

"Quite decent, indeed. Congratulations. The thought quickly came and went that maybe the client was Ben, but she decided to say nothing.

He seemed so different. Relaxed. And he didn't pull out a handkerchief once.

"You look good. New hairstyle, I see," he said, meaning it as a compliment.

"I've had about three since you've seen me. You like it?"

"Very attractive."

"Thank you."

Because she didn't know what to say, she was actually silent for one of the few times in her life. She wished he would say something. Take the lead.

And then he said something. Something rather profound. "Would you say yes if I asked you out sometime? Dinner? A movie? I didn't plan on saying that. It just came out."

She was surprised. "You can take it back. Just forget you ever said it. We'll never bring it up again." Again. That was just as bad. Hadn't she been thinking of asking him the same question?

"I don't want to take it back."

"This is really quite a civilized divorce, isn't it? I guess it's all about timing. The truth is, earlier, I was thinking of you. And then you appeared. Gotta mean something, don't you think?"

He didn't answer.

"Don't you think?" She was a little nervous. She felt a lot of things with Ben, but she had never felt nervous.

"I think you should know I've been seeing a therapist."

"Oh." Here it comes. First he asks her out, then he tells her he's seeing another woman. Was he here to tell her he was getting married? "Oh," she said again. So the apartment deal was for them. What a fool she was to think it was for any other reason. "Well, goody for you. I mean really congratulations. Really. I mean it. I'm not dating anyone." Shut up, Brenda. You sound like a jerk.

"You think—? No, no, no, not like that. Professionally seeing."

It took a second or two for Brenda to get it. "Oh, like a psychotherapist. "She put great emphasis on the *psycho* part. "Oh, I see. But why? You were always the normal one. Sort of."

"Because I want to know why I screwed up a marriage with the woman I love."

He had said 'marriage with' and not 'marriage to' and for some reason, this had great significance. This was Ben, but he wasn't talking like Ben. And he hadn't used his handkerchief once. She decided to spill it all. Get it out in the open. She guided him to the couch and they sat.

"It took two marriages, two divorces, a few affairs for me to figure it out," she said. "I've really been out there. Went wild after you left. After you and I split. Did things I only used to write about. You know what I mean?" She had never intended to give him the intimate details, but it just came out that way. And why not? She didn't have to feel guilty about anything. It wasn't like she was cheating on him. It all happened when they were divorced.

"You're a writer. You were exploring. It was for research."

He never would have said that before when they were married. He would have stormed out of the room or maybe the apartment. She looked at his face again just to make sure it really was Ben. Is this where she should tell him how much she missed him? How lonely it was in that apartment without him? That maybe she did love him, had always loved him. That she was the one who should be in therapy.

She didn't say any of those things. She said, "Maybe, but all I learned is I'm weird; not too swift; superficial." She smiled. They were talking. They were really talking. She got up and poured herself another glass of wine.

"Join me?"

"You're not weird; you're very bright; you're very genuine. Come back and sit next to me. I didn't know you drank in the daytime."

"Any time. I like it. But only when I'm writing. It helps." She sat down, this time a little closer to him.

"I miss the part of me that was when I was with you."

"The part of you that was when you were with me. Yes. That's what we really mean when we say 'I miss you' to someone. I've tried to do so many other things—well, I have done so many other things. I found out how much you're a part of me."

"Do you think we could try again? I'll re-phrase that. Do you want to try again?"

"I want to be sure you're sure. That you mean it." Not even she could write dialogue this good. She started to take another sip of her wine, but didn't. She was sure she was going to need both hands for what was coming next. She put the glass of wine down on the end table.

"I'm sure, Brenda."

"This is what I think. You go away now, and if you feel the same tomorrow or the next day or any time, I'll be waiting for you. I've never had an affair with an ex-husband. It's time I did. But I'm not exactly sure of the logistics."

"I'm not talking about an affair," he said earnestly.

"Neither am I," she said looking into his eyes. She reached for his hand and put it against her cheek.

The old was new. She liked it. But this was better. She liked the boy. She liked the girl. She liked it all. Mother was right. She could have avoided a lot of heartbreak if she had just listened to her.

He looked long and hard.

"What?" she said.

"Just looking," he said.

"If I asked you to stay tonight," she said, "would you?"

"But I thought you said go away, see how I feel tomorrow. I know how I'm going to feel tomorrow. And if you ask me to stay tonight, I'll say yes."

And very slowly, very very slowly, very tenderly, they wrapped themselves around one another.

"This time I'm not letting go. I'll be good this time, Ben. I swear I'll be good. I won't let you down."

"Be any way you want to be. Just be Brenda. Just be my Brenda."

She teared up.

"Sweetheart, you're crying." He took out his handkerchief and wiped her eyes. "Why are you sad? This is good. Isn't this good?"

"No, not sad. Happy. Happiness." She was never so glad to see his handkerchief.

And then he started to cry.

"I don't think I've ever seen you cry," she said. She had her true love back and this time it would be right. This was real. This wasn't fiction. She'd been out there and it wasn't what she wanted. She did at the time; thought she did; but not anymore.

"Why do we have to go away to find out what we have is what we wanted all along?"

"My mother used to say everything we want and need is in our own backyard."

"Wise mother."

"She always said you were the one for me. I listened, but I wanted to defy her. So I didn't hear. There's a lot of unfinished business between mothers and daughters."

"What about now? Us."

"Mother knew best."

"Good girl."

"Ben?"

"Yes?"

"This may be bad timing, but I have to say it. You haven't blown your nose once. I mean we're using your handkerchief to wipe our eyes; you haven't sniffed or sniveled."

"I'm seeing a nutritionist. Seems the problem is my diet. Or was. This handkerchief is just for show."

She was not going to say she told him so. "Seems there have been a lot of changes. For both of us."

"And I have a personal trainer. Don. Working on Qi Gong now. It's fantastic. All about the energy. A gentle form of Tai Chi. You'll have to get into it."

She didn't want to grow old alone. She wanted to make all the mistakes and have all the good times with Ben. All the ups and down. All the way, like the song says. She thought about her mother, the hand that rocks the cradle, who always said that Ben was the kind you stay with because he's the kind who stays. What more could a good girl want?

Mr. Gordon was home. Mrs. Gordon was home. Mr. and Mrs. Gordon sat on the living room couch crying and laughing sharing one handkerchief. Sometimes a handkerchief is just a handkerchief. Freud 101.

Not young, not old, Brenda Gordon was in the afternoon of her life. And everyone knows the sun is hottest in the afternoon.

End

SUSAN SURMAN

Susan Surman—aka Susan Kramer/Gracie Luck—lived and worked in London for 23 years. Her performing credits include London's West End, Edinburgh, the Sydney Opera House, Ensemble Theatre, BBC radio, TV, and film. Writing credits include material for Tracey Ullman, two plays performed (one commissioned for TV), and a play and a screenplay optioned. After her return to the USA, she focused on writing fiction weaving in her extensive background in acting and travel. Ask her where she gets her ideas and she will say, "Why invent? All I have to do is remember."

She lives in North Carolina.